Lingering Laughter

Georgina Grey

FAWCETT COVENTRY • NEW YORK

LINGERING LAUGHTER

Published by Fawcett Coventry Books, CBS Educational and Professional Publishing, a division of CBS Inc.

ISBN: 0-449-50273-2

Printed in the United States of America

First Fawcett Coventry printing: March 1982

10 9 8 7 6 5 4 3 2 1

For Kinley

chapter one

"*My dear, you must remember that there are fortune hunters everywhere!*" Lady Blunder declared as they waited for the sedan chairs which were to take them down the steep slope of Gay Street to the Pump Room where they would take the waters. "Bath is notorious for being full of them, which means that you must take care."

"But I have no fortune, Aunt," Jenny protested cheerfully. "As soon as news of that gets about, I shall not have to worry."

By no stretch of the imagination could Lady Blunder be called a pretty woman. Tall and angular of build, with a beaklike nose and myopic eyes which were often fastened in a squint, she was a familiar sight about the city and, indeed, was famous for her bon mots and various eccentricities.

"But, my dear child, of course it cannot be put about that you have no dowry!" she exclaimed. "Do you want to frighten away all the eligible gentlemen straight away?"

"But you have just warned me about fortune hunters, Aunt," the girl protested. "And now you say I should pretend to have a dowry in order to attract a husband. Somehow that seems a contradiction."

"I have never cared for conundrums," Lady Blunder told her. "In particular my own. La, there are our chairs at last, child."

When she saw two sets of four men advancing, each group carrying an enclosed chair set on poles, Jenny's heart sank. She had no wish to tuck herself into a dank and mildewed box and be carried down to the center of the city. It was her first day in the famous spa, and she would much rather have walked down Gay Street to the Pump Room, no matter how steep the hill. But she made no protest even though it was a fine, sunny day and she could see the river sparkling below and the green hills folding into one another beyond.

After all, she owed her aunt and uncle so much for inviting her to join them at this delightful place. After her widowed mother's death, Jenny had been taken in by an elderly cousin in Manchester for a year. But when she had reached eighteen it had been decided that she should make something approximating a coming out, despite her lack of dowry, and with this end in mind she had been sent to live with her maiden aunt and equally unmarried uncle in Bath.

"We would have had you straight away, my dear," Sir Simon had told Jenny when she had arrived by coach at the White Hart Inn the day before, "but my sister would have it that this is a dangerous place for a young girl to be, and I have been all these months persuading her that you are not likely to be ravished on the North Parade."

All of which was a rather startling introduction, although it helped to prepare Jenny for her aunt's peculiar turn of mind which made her fancy that dangers lurked everywhere in Society to beset maidens under twenty-five.

"Oh dear, you are not only young but you are beautiful as well!" had been Lady Blunder's wail when she had first set eyes upon her niece. "A year ago you were simply pretty, and I had not planned to cope with more."

It had not occurred to Jenny before that she was a more than ordinarily attractive girl. She saw nothing particularly arresting about her black curls which she had let grow long, and certainly her eyes were an ordinary blue, although perhaps more thickly fringed than most. Indeed, in her opinion, her nose was not as long as it should be and her lips rather fuller than she would prefer. But she had seen at once that Lady Blunder was not the sort to be contradicted in anything, even when she was clearly wrong, which was more likely to be the case than not.

However that might be, Lady Blunder had spent the evening of Jenny's arrival warning her of all the hazards life in Bath presented.

"The strict rules which govern society in London are not to be found here, you must understand," she had declared as they sat before the fire in a charming little sitting room with Sir Simon snoring in his wing chair at the side. "Everyone comes here to take the waters, and, as a consequence, you will be required to rub elbows with the hoi polloi wherever you go."

Jenny made the decision not to remind her aunt that that would be no novelty to her, deciding that was not the sort of thing Lady Blunder would want to be reminded of. A year ago, when she and her brother had attended Jenny's mother's funeral, Lady Blunder had made it clear enough that she considered that her sister had made a sorry choice when she had chosen to marry the second son of a country vicar who had decided to follow in his father's footsteps. It did not seem to enter her mind that it might possibly have happened that Jenny's mother had been very happy, and Jenny had been too full of sorrow at her loss to explain how full her mother's life had been. And now she saw that Lady Blunder was determined to put the best face on her background in order to provide for a successful coming out. It had been then, with the fire hissing in the hearth, that Jenny had determined never to lie about her past, no matter what her aunt decided to do.

"La, you will meet squires and merchants and every sort of common person," her aunt had continued, warming to her subject. "The price of subscriptions are so modest that anyone can afford to come here to attend the concerts and even the balls at Harrison's and Lindsey's Rooms. And as for the Pump Room and the gardens, they are quite free."

Jenny had taken that occasion to suggest that perhaps there was nothing so very wrong in it.

"My dear child!" her aunt had cried. "Why, you are a perfect innocent if you do not realize what sorts of practices all this gives rise to. Professional gamesters who the members of the *haut ton* would not enter the same room with in London come to Bath and arrange for gambling in private houses. Private parties of such a sort are supposed to be banned, but they are not. Even Nash himself, when he was still alive and Master of Ceremonies here, could not entirely control high play."

At that point Jenny had ventured to suggest that she might not be affected by this particular peril since she played no other game but whist.

"But it *does* lower that general tone, this gambling with anyone," Lady Blunder had insisted. "Simon will agree with me, I know."

And, leaning forward, she rapped her brother vigorously on the knee with her folded fan.

"Damme, what is it, Tabitha?" Sir Simon demanded petulantly. "You know I need a little nap of an evening when we are at home in order to prepare myself for bed."

Jenny had found her uncle to be a gentleman intent on having a degree of peace and quiet, which his sister persisted in making quite impossible. "You'll find me a moderate fellow, my dear," he had told her at their first meeting at the White Hart Inn, and nothing she had seen since had indicated differently. In appearance, however, he was very like his sister with the same hooked nose and narrowed eyes, although the effect, somehow, was not at all the same. Whereas Lady Blunder was far from handsome, there was something singularly attractive about Sir Simon.

"I asked you if the constant gambling does not lower the general tone of Bath," Jenny's aunt demanded now, ingoring the rebuke. "I was telling Jenny that all sorts of people come down from London."

"'Sdeath, you will make the gel wonder why it is we choose to keep a house here," Sir Simon grumbled. "Do not believe half of what she tells you, my dear, and you will do very well indeed."

"Why, as for keeping a house here," Lady Blunder declared, demonstrating once again that she would not stoop to acknowledge any criticism which her brother might provide, "where else should we be when all of London comes here at some time or other during the year? But that does not mean the city is safe for young gels, Simon. And who will warn her if I do not?"

But Sir Simon did not answer the question, having fallen back to sleep while his sister was talking.

"I will confess that gambling may not affect you," Lady Blunder continued with a shrug of resignation. "But there is a general atmosphere of informality about the place which I believe is quite infectious if you do not guard against it. Ladies and gentlemen who would not be seen abroad in London without being dressed in the pink of fashion will go out in public here in their dressing gowns if they are on their way to the baths."

Jenny had assumed the expected expression of amazement and smoothed the pink muslin of one of a number of new gowns her aunt had presented her with on her arrival. Clearly Lady Blunder was a generous person and kind as well, and if she *would* fret about the sorry influences there was very little Jenny could do to stop her. At the very least, she owed her the respect shown by close attention.

And yet sometimes that evening her mind had wandered, particularly when she wondered, not for the first time, what her mother would have wanted her to do, whether or not she would have had her come here. She had been a gentle soul, but very proud, and not close at all to the brother and sister who were so much older than herself. And she would accept no financial assistance, either from her father when he had still been alive or from her brother when he had inherited the title and the modest fortune which accompanied it. She had chosen the simple life, she said, and, although she never had condemned the more frivolous existence of her brother and sister, she had made it clear that it held little interest for her.

Probably, Jenny thought, she would have made an alliance with someone like the curate, had her mother only lived and not been struck down so suddenly, and have lived the sort of quiet life her parents had. But now that she was here in Bath she found that she was more excited than she had imagined she would be and that her aunt's recitation of the perils she must avoid only whetted her curiosity.

"Why, at any number of the baths gentlemen are admitted as well as ladies!" Lady Blunder declared. "Yes, my dear, that is quite true! Of course, everyone is well covered with canvas wear, but that does not prevent me from disapproving. If you decide to test the mineral water, you must go to Queen's Bath, which is for ladies only."

Jenny had assured her aunt that she would remember that and wondered whether every evening spent at home would be filled with so much good advice.

"La, there are no end of things a gel like yourself must keep in mind," Lady Blunder continued. "There is the schedule, for one thing. Between eight and nine of a morning, everyone visits the Pump Room to drink the water. Dr. Dangle prescribes three glasses. But the main thing, of course, is to meet one's friends. It is especially important, my dear, to be seen in the proper place at the proper time. I know your uncle will agree with me."

And once again she struck her brother such a blow with her fan that he sprang straight out of his seat as though propelled by exploding powder.

"Damme, Tabitha!" he shouted. "One day you will be the death of me!"

And, straightening the black horsehair wig which he affected when at home, he strode out of the sitting room in high dudgeon, the tails of his long coat flapping.

"What a temper the man has!" Jenny's aunt exclaimed. "I declare that even though I expect to worry about you constantly, I am glad enough to have you here of an evening when there is no entertainment. Simon is no company, as you can see, at least when his only alternative is to talk to *me*. But when you see him at the Assembly Rooms tomorrow evening it will be quite another story, I assure you, for he fancies himself a ladies' man when properly encouraged, and a certain Lady Carew has...But that is by the by. I was speaking of proper place and proper time."

The day had started early for Jenny, and the journey to Bath had been long and bumpy. As a consequence, she had wanted nothing more than to follow her uncle's lead and fall asleep. But she had listened to a recitation of a list of events to be attended which, had she had anything at all to say, would have left her speechless. Following the early visit to the Pump Room, it appeared, there were bookshops to be attended.

"Some will go to a coffeehouse at that hour," her aunt had told her, "but it is no place for a young gel like yourself. Why, you would hear all manner of conversations on politics, philosophy and scandal which are quite beyond you!"

After the visit to the bookseller's, Jenny discovered, they would pass some time at the milliner's looking at hats and then, more often than not, stop at Mr. Gill's, the pastry cook, for a jelly or a tart. Or perhaps, if the day were fine, cross the river by boat to a certain grove called Spring Garden, which, her aunt assured her, was a sweet retreat of walks and flowers, not to mention breakfasting and ballrooms.

"At midday we go to church at the Abbey. Dinner is taken at three. A retirement follows before the evening's activities begin. Balls twice a week. Concerts every other night. And there are plays performed in a theater beneath Simpson's Rooms. You see, my dear, how busy we shall be. Busy enough to keep you out of mischief, I think."

And, although Jenny had declared quite firmly that she had not come to Bath to look for mischief, her aunt had shaken her turbaned head knowingly and placed one finger beside her nose.

"If it were not for your good looks I would not worry," she said. "Unless, of course, you had a fortune. Which reminds me..."

But Jenny had pleaded weariness, and whatever Lady Blunder had meant to say was forgotten. But this morning it had come to mind, and, not content with one reminder, she made two.

"I have put it about, you see, that you lack for nothing," she declared as the sedan chairs were deposited in front of them by two sets of four puffing fellows who, having made the ascent of the hill, had now to descend it with an added burden.

"You did not say that I was rich!" Jenny cried, distressed.

"I did not take the trouble to be specific," her aunt replied. "People will think what they please. That is why I saw fit to warn you just now about fortune hunters."

And with that Lady Blunder got inside her sedan chair, not without some difficulty on account of her extreme height.

"Come along, my dear," she called out the window. "If we do not hurry, we will not be at the Pump Room until nine."

chapter two

The Pump Room was so crowded that Jenny wondered how they would ever get inside, but here her aunt's height proved a positive advantage since, standing head and shoulders over nearly everyone, she was able to see the spot where they should move to next. Never, Jenny thought, had she seen so many invalids gathered together in one spot, gout appearing to be the primary affliction. There were nearly as many canes as there were feet, and several portly gentlemen were being wheeled about in Bath chairs to the extreme discomfort of everyone they passed.

There was a counter in one corner on which glasses were set, and it was to this counter that Lady Blunder steered her niece. They were each poured a glass of spring water by a mob-capped lass who laughed when Jenny puckered up her lips after her first taste.

"It is not to everyone's fancy, Miss," she said, "but it will do you good, or so the doctors say."

"This city is full of doctors, quacks of all varieties," Lady Blunder declared. "Except, of course, for dear Dr. Dangle who can always be relied on. Look about you, child. Did you ever see such a motley crowd in all your life? Now you understand why I have warned you to be discriminate in your acquaintances."

And, indeed, Jenny thought she had never seen such a strange assortment of people ever in her life. And nearly everyone, halt or lame or in good health, was in such dishabille as to make her aunt's proper morning costume, a grey taffeta sacque with scarlet trimmings, and Jenny's own white polonaise with its small hoop and green apron seem like formal wear.

"I would never come here in my dressing gown!" her aunt exclaimed in honest outrage. "Never! Of course with your uncle it is quite another matter. He claims not to follow fashion, but I notice that his inclinations always lead him in the same direction fashion moves."

It was difficult for Jenny to imagine Sir Simon in undress, but when she made more particular inquiry her aunt declared that he had preceded them to the center of the town that morning.

"And when I last saw him getting into a sedan chair, he was certainly in his dressing gown," she told the girl. "And at this very moment I expect that he is in the King's Bath. Here. It is just below this window. Pardon us, Madam. Allow me to pass, Sir. Yes! There he is."

The circular stone bath below them was nearly as crowded as the Pump Room, and in the very middle of its steaming waters Sir Simon could be seen, immersed to his chin, his bald head shining in the morning sunlight. About him gentlemen and ladies gamboled, the former pushing little floating dishes in front of them in which they kept their handkerchief or snuff or, in one case, a nosegay.

Jenny started as she heard her aunt suck in her breath. "And there *she* is!" she exclaimed in a low voice. "How she flaunts herself! And what delight he takes in her excessive admiration!"

"And who is that?" Jenny asked.

Lady Blunder's expression was a dreadful thing to see. "Lady Carew," she hissed. "The hussy has been pursuing him for weeks. One would never have thought that her husband has not been dead a year. I declare, I cannot abide the jade, and her daughter Letty is an impertinent chit with perfectly disgraceful ways. Why, last Tuesday night at the Assembly Rooms at Simpson's, I saw her flirting with the son of a common ironmonger and her mother looking on, all smiles, as though nothing were the matter."

By straining to the left, Jenny was able to see

that there was a lady in the water rather closer to her uncle than strict delicacy might have thought quite proper. But her curiosity to see the face of this lady who had so incurred her aunt's disfavor could not be satisfied, thanks to the large, puffed green cap she was wearing to protect her hair from the water.

"Such indelicacy!" Lady Blunder sniffed. "But what can I do, my dear? I am living in your uncle's house. I cannot refuse even to receive her. Sometimes I think he leads her on just to annoy me! If only people would behave properly.... Ah, Dr. Dangle! I was just making mention of you! You must meet my niece, Jenny, who I told you was coming to join us here in Bath. It is a great responsibility. I feel it here!"

And, pressing one hand to her bosom and the other to her head, she left the company in doubt as to the precise location of the sensation.

Jenny was bewildered by her first sight of Dr. Dangle, for if anyone had ever looked a quack, he did. He was a little man, scarcely taller than herself, and his face was as red as the hair beneath his periwig, so red, in fact, that had it not been for his profession Jenny might have taken him for a topper. Indeed, there was a particularly lurching manner to his movement which heightened the effect. And, although what she smelled on his person might have been sal volatile, it might just as well have been gin.

"I make a prescription of assafoetida drops, two taken every hour," he declared in a grand manner. "The fee for this consultation is a guinea, and I will send your brother a bill."

Which business having been so efficiently concluded, he bowed to Jenny who was able to determine, now that he was close, that his clothing was in a singular state of disarray, the attempt at making up his cravat having clearly gone awry, not to mention other evidences that his toilette had not been made with a steady hand.

"Miss Allen!" he declared, swaying ever so slightly to the left as he recovered from his bow. "I have heard a deal about you. One look is sufficient to assure me that it was high time you came to Bath. Note the color of her cheeks, Lady Blunder."

"Why, she is only a little flushed from the crowd and the heat," Jenny's aunt replied, albeit frowning and squinting up her eyes the better to see her niece's complexion.

"There is more to it than that, I think," Dr. Dangle announced in a pontificating manner which made several people in their vicinity turn to stare at him. "Let me take your pulse, my dear."

And, before Jenny could prevent it, he had taken her wrist and was holding it to his right ear!

"I have my own methods in everything," he explained when several bystanders demanded what he was about. "Some physicians *feel* the heartbeat. I prefer to feel *and* hear it. Lady

Blunder will assure you that I am nothing if not thorough."

"Oh, yes, dear Dr. Dangle, you are quite unique," Jenny's aunt declared. "One can always depend on you for the unexpected."

"Including the diagnosis!" a young blood standing near suggested to the general merriment of the crowd. Close to him a dark gentleman in riding dress smiled a sardonic smile.

As for Jenny, she was torn between embarrassment and amusement. It was difficult enough to hear what anyone was saying in·this room, not to mention having anyone listen for a heartbeat. She wondered how her aunt ever could have allowed herself to be taken in by such a fellow. It was an ironic thought given the pains the older woman had put herself to to warn Jenny about charlatans.

"Aha!" Dr. Dangle declared. "Just as I supposed! I detect a murmur! This will be even a more difficult case than I first supposed. If you will take my word, Miss Allen, you will drink three of the larger glasses of mineral water every morning before ten. I will make further prescription this afternoon at four when I come to make my daily visit. Until then, ladies, goodbye."

And with that he turned so abruptly that he nearly lost his balance and went lurching off, clutching for something in the deep pocket of his wrinkled coat. By standing on tiptoe, Jenny was just able to see him take out a small bottle which, she must suppose, contained his own medicine, for the doctor held it to his mouth and must have consumed the entire contents before floundering off, wiping his mouth on his coat sleeve. A general merriment in the crowd ensued, but Lady Blunder did not appear to notice.

"Such a clever man," she declared complacently. "Why, he gives me such exclusive service that I am never completely well. He attends me every day at four, just as you heard him say, and now you will be his patient, as well. There is no need to worry about being restricted as to activity, for the one thing Doctor Dangle never suggests is bed rest, except for special patients. Indeed, I have often heard him say that it is the very worst thing since it is his conviction that the blood must be kept stirring about during the day."

"And does he prescribe for my uncle, as well?" Jenny inquired, making a silent resolve not to become Dr. Dangle's patient no matter what her aunt might say.

"Oh, I have no patience with your uncle!" Lady Blunder declared, looking down at the King's Bath where Sir Simon could still be seen basking in the watery attentions of Lady Carew. "He has the most unkind things to say about the dear doctor. But you must not listen to him, my dear. He is no judge if character such as I am. La! There is Lady Madrigal, surrounded by admirers as usual. We must try to edge our way into the circle so that you may be presented."

And so they hove their way to a corner where an extraordinarily stout personage wearing a feathered turban and a *robe à l'anglaise*, the cut of which made her look even more excessive than she was, was holding court. Indeed, the expressions on the faces of the ladies and gentlemen about her—most of them of a certain age—was so sycophantic as to create the impression that she was some sort of monstrous Diana descended from the Olympian heights.

"Lady Madrigal's private entertainments are the most popular in Bath," Lady Blunder told Jenny. "Everyone who is invited must be prepared to give a musical rendition of some sort, either on an instrument such as the violin or harpsichord or singing. Whistling is acceptable on occasion. The only line drawn is against bagpipes. As dear Devina says, we must draw limits somewhere. And, believe me, my dear, in artistic circles, Devina's word is law."

As soon as they were noticed—and Lady Blunder could never be ignored for long, if for no other reason than her height and commanding expression—Lady Madrigal condescended to them in the most affable way imaginable.

"You must bring your niece to our little soirée on Wednesday," she declared, smiling beneficently as the waters of her admirers parted to let them through. "I was just telling dear Sir Timity that we will expect him to play on the lute. That will balance Mr. Littlejohn's performance on the kettledrum very nicely, I believe.

And, of course, we have a special treat. Lady Andrews on the jew's-harp. Tell me, my dear, what instrument do you play?"

Jenny was accomplished on the pianoforte, but she was not prepared to admit it until she had attended one of Lady Madrigal's musical entertainments. The lute was well enough, but she did not think the combination of kettledrum and jew's-harp was promising, and so she avoided a direct answer, which was a very easy thing to do given that Lady Madrigal rarely listened to anything anyone else had to say.

"Sir Timity is a bachelor!" Lady Blunder whispered in Jenny's ear, which information given suddenly so startled the girl that she found herself flushing as her aunt performed still another introduction. And it was no help to find that the dark gentleman who had observed her encounter with Dr. Dangle was still keeping her in view. This time he was leaning nonchalantly against a nearby column, and there was no doubt as to his amusement, although he stopped smiling as soon as Jenny indignantly caught his eye.

Sir Timity was, Lady Blunder explained, a dear friend and one of the finest musicians imaginable. "To hear him play his lute and sing, my dear, is certain heaven," she said looming over the gentleman in question in an amiable way.

"Dear lady!" Sir Timity protested. "You quite

embarrass me. Delightful to meet you, Miss Allen! If you will allow me..."

And, before Jenny could prevent it, he had kissed her fingers in a lingering sort of way, all the time keeping his eyes, which were blue and watery, on her as though he could not bear to look away.

Sir Timity was not prepossessing in appearance no matter what his musical ability. Granted that every effort had been made by artifice to accomplish a transformation. His height had been increased by the wearing of red high-heeled shoes, and his pantaloons were cut as low as fashion would allow to prevent too close a scrutiny of his scrawny shanks. His waistcoat was an amazing affair of embroidered satin, and the skirts of his coat had somehow been stiffened in a way to make it appear that there was more of him. An elaborately tied cravat did its best to hide a scrawny throat, although his Adam's apple kept escaping. As for the face itself, it might well have belonged to a consumptive, so white and drawn did it appear. Other than that, he seemed an ordinary enough fellow, although to listen to Lady Blunder one would think he was the most sought-after gentleman in Bath. Indeed, the atmosphere of congratulation appeared to be mutual.

"You should be very proud of your aunt, Miss Allen," Sir Timity declared in a shrill voice which carried even further than that of Lady Madrigal, who had returned her attention to

27

her circle of admirers. "She is the master of the bon mot. Has she told you? Every day a new amusing saying. Come, Lady Blunder. What is the witticism for today to be?"

"Shall I confess something to you, Sir Timity?" Jenny's aunt replied, clearly delighted by the compliment. "I never really know until I have said it. That is, I simply go about the day in my usual way and I am certain to say something amusing. It is quite involuntary. My particular method of composition. And, do you know, it often happens that I have no idea that what I have said is the least bit amusing until people begin to laugh. And that is how my bon mots come into being, Sir. It will be a secret between us."

"A secret that your lovely niece must share," Sir Timity declared in a voice which made Jenny want to cover up her ears. She wondered if the dark gentleman was listening and hoped that he had gone away. She could not endure being laughed at and had turned her back on him so as not to have to see. She was aware of her inability sometimes to keep her temper, and she certainly did not want to flare up at a stranger on her first full day in Bath.

"Heiresses are not often quite so beautiful," Sir Timity continued with a smile which only succeeded in making him look like a death's head.

"I am not an heiress, I assure you," Jenny

replied, glancing accusingly at her aunt. "You have been incorrectly informed."

He laughed at that. "Oh, I was told you would protest, my dear," he said, still in that carrying voice. "Your aunt explained that you would make a secret of it. And, of course, that is very wise. There are all sorts of unscrupulous people about, often of the middle class. Money is all they think of, and if they believe you to be without a shilling, all the better. But it does no harm to have those you trust know the truth."

"Sir Timity is one of my most intimate friends," Lady Blunder explained.

"Someone you trust completely, like Dr. Dangle," Jenny suggested.

"Just so, my dear! She is so quick, Sir Timity. And she is proving an able student of the ways of Society at Bath."

"Your aunt is a fine judge of character, Miss Allen," Sir Timity said with a smirk.

"I can see she is, Sir," Jenny said and made to turn away, only to have her eyes meet those of the mocking gentleman. And this time he made no attempt to hide his smile of clear amusement.

chapter three

Accustomed as she was to nothing more brilliant than country dances performed to the music of a single fiddler in the village hall, Jenny could not but be impressed by the glitter and excitement which the Assembly Rooms presented that evening. Three circular rooms surrounded by Greek-columned walls gave off at regular intervals to a large ballroom with musicians mounted on a platform. And how the place was crowded! No longer in their morning dishabille, the ladies sparkled like so many jewels, their powdered hair done so uncommonly high that had Jenny not observed at first hand her aunt's abigail, Gertrude, busily building a mound on Lady Blunder's head which, in fact, consisted primarily of wool, she would have been at a loss to explain how those cleverly coiffured edifices would remain in place, decorated as they were not only with bows and ribbons and feathers, too, but some with toy-sized replicas of ships in sail and every sort of thing.

As for the gentlemen, they were only less startling arrayed in that their heads went undecorated except for powder. As for their costumes, they were elaborate enough with coats of satin in every color, embroidered waistcoats, and so much lace dripping from their sleeves as to make one think them all refugees from Brussels. Even Sir Simon, although on the whole more modestly costumed, had taken such pains with his cravat that the lower part of his face was scarcely visible.

"Now, my dear," Lady Blunder declared as they made their way toward the ballroom, "you must take advice from me in everything. If a gentleman should present himself and you find me pulling my left ear, you may take the floor with him. But if I tap my nose with my fan, you must plead a previous engagement. Appearances at these affairs are calculated to lead young gels astray, for there is no telling the finery of a gentleman from that of the commoner sort down from London to seek their prey."

And, with that advice, she assumed an expression which would not have been out of place had they been in the wilds of Africa.

"Let the poor girl alone, Tabby," Sir Simon exclaimed with a broad smile, which was barely visible from underneath his flowing cravat.

"You will make her think she is in danger of abduction or worse. I cannot think what harm can come to her here, 'pon my soul I can't."

"That is because you have no imagination," Lady Blunder replied in a snappish sort of way, her temper not improved, no doubt, by the buffeting they were receiving on all sides by the company about them, which seemed to be making a concerted rush in the direction of the dance floor. "Harm could come to her reputation, I assure you, as you ought to know very well. It must be established at once that she has discrimination!"

"Why, as for that…" Sir Simon began, clearly intent on argument, only to be interrupted by a lady of a certain age with a coy manner and bold blue eyes who appeared from nowhere to clutch him by the arm.

"Why, Lady Carew!" Lady Blunder said stiffly. "I had not dared to hope that we would see you this evening."

"I cannot think why you should have come to that conclusion, my dear," the other replied. "You know quite well how I dote on these Tuesday evenings. Indeed, I told Sir Simon this morning at the bath that we would be certain to see one another."

Lady Blunder assumed a sour expression, while Sir Simon beamed in the way in which any gentleman of advancing years might do when complimented by a pretty woman's attentions. Meanwhile, Lady Carew reached out and pulled a young girl, distinguished mainly by her flaming red curls and cheerful smile, from the surging crowd.

"My dear," Lady Carew said to Jenny, "I know you must be the niece your uncle has so often spoken to me of. This is my daughter, Letty. I am certain that you will be the best of friends."

Lady Blunder scowled in such a way as to indicate that if they were it would not be with her blessing, but Jenny returned Letty's smile. In an instant, thanks perhaps to Lady Carew's maneuvering, the two girls found their little party separated, with Sir Simon and the mother on their way toward the dance floor where a cotillion group was forming and Lady Blunder completely out of sight.

"How cleverly Mama has arranged for us to be alone together!" Letty exclaimed, taking Jenny's arm. "She said to me earlier that you would not have much enjoyment this evening with your aunt playing watchdog, as I am quite certain that she should. We shall do much better on our own."

Jenny considered. Doubtless what Letty said was true. There had been no question in Jenny's mind that her aunt would hover and advise. Still, she had been prepared for the worst. And, in a way, she did not mind. Although a single morning spent in her aunt's company at the Pump Room had been quite enough to convince her that Lady Blunder was not an ace when it came to character evaluation, she had found it all amusing. Or might have if she had not glimpsed that mocking fellow who clearly thought her aunt, and the people she surrounded herself with, absurd. Furthermore, she did not want the older woman to worry.

On the other hand, if she were to refuse Letty's invitation to go off on their own she might be renouncing the chance of a proper friendship. The one thing she had missed since coming to Bath was the fellowship of someone her own age. Granted her aunt had promised her a youthful abigail, but Jenny did not think that would be quite the same thing. And there was another reason for keeping Letty company, and that was her desire to see Bath through eyes which had not grown as cynical as her aunt's. How she cast her lot in life might well depend on the attitudes she developed here. She was a sensible girl and she knew that.

"You are concerned she will be worried," Letty announced, drawing her into an alcove. "Quite right, too, no doubt. Mama is thoughtless sometimes and I am, too. And in Mama's case there is the added incentive to irritate your aunt because she knows she disapproves of her. Mama is very fond of your uncle, as you may have noticed. Indeed," she added brightly, "so am I. He is a perfect poppet."

Jenny had not thought of Sir Simon in quite that light before, but now that Letty had said it she thought it might be true. Until now she had thought of him as a moderating influence in the household. But no doubt he was something quite otherwise to Letty and her mother. Jenny wondered just how far the affair with Lady Carew had gone.

"Still," Letty continued, returning to the subject under consideration, "if we go and find your aunt, she will find some way of separating us, and I would like to have you for a friend. She thinks that I am frivolous, you see. And she is perfectly correct! I flirt, as well, quite shamelessly. And Lady Blunder disapproves. Worst of all, I am not careful of the company I keep. That is to say, I do not consult the *Almanach de Gotha* before I accept a gentleman's offer to fetch me punch."

There was one thing about Letty, Jenny thought. She did not care whether she elicited response. "I have such an idea!" she cried now. "We will both take to the floor with perfectly proper gentlemen. They are all dull, but no matter. There is one over there. Sir Roger Ramsdale. The one with hair sprouting out both ears. And he is talking to the Honorable Tommy Basset. Your aunt is certain to approve of *him* for he dotes on Lady Madrigal's musical evenings. I believe he plays the castanets his father brought back from Spain, or something of the sort. Your aunt will see you with him on the floor, and her mind will be put instantly at ease. Only let me arrange your dress."

Jenny's gown was of pink and silver taffeta

35

pulled up in bunches at the side and back to reveal a rich, red underskirt, but it was modest in its cut. Too modest for Letty's taste apparently because, before Jenny knew what she was about, the girl had tugged at her bodice.

"More décolletage is needed," Letty explained. "Yes, that is more exciting."

"But I thought you said these two gentlemen we are to snare were of the conservative sort," Jenny replied, not troubling to hide her amusement while Letty struggled with her own gown, which was cut quite low enough as it was.

"When we are whirling about the floor we are an advertisement of ourselves," her friend explained. "A good many gentlemen will watch us, and not all of them will be as conservative as our partners. There! Do you understand me?"

"I think I do," Jenny replied dryly, readjusting her bodice to its original position. "Well, we will advertise ourselves in different ways. I will make a compromise of it and dance with Mr. Basset. But first, I think, he must ask me. And soon since the cotillion line is nearly formed."

"Oh, there is nothing to that!" Letty exclaimed, and in a flash she managed, by a flutter of her fan and eyes combined together with a curling smile, to attract the attention of the two young gentlemen, who hurried to her side. In an instant introductions were performed and, as though by magic, a giggling Letty was being led onto the floor by the hirsute-eared Sir Roger and Jenny was on the Honorable Tommy Basset's arm.

They had no sooner taken their position than the musicians struck up a tune. Jenny was able to make her way through the figures gracefully without entering into conversation with her partner, who was distinguished by such a pasty white complexion that it might have been thought he never ventured out of doors. His expression could not have been more complimentary, however, and it was clear he thought himself a lucky fellow. As for Jenny, her mind and conscience were relieved when she saw her aunt waving to her from the sidelines and looking very satisfied indeed.

But when the cotillion was over, Jenny looked for her aunt in vain. The crush had become so great, in fact, that movement was nearly impossible, with the result that she found herself trying to make conversation with Mr. Basset, who, when threatened with such intimacy, turned red and stammered, not to mention shifting from foot to foot in a disconcerting sort of way. Even the subject of castanets failed to move him to fluency, and Jenny was near to despairing when Letty, who had disappeared the moment the dance had ended, made her appearance with a gentleman who bore no likeness to Sir Roger Ramsdale at her side. Indeed, it was no other than the mocking gentleman with the disturbing dark eyes whom Jenny had seen that morning at the Pump Room.

"Do fetch some punch, Tommy, there's a dear!" Letty declared in a breezy manner. "Jenny, this gentleman is a friend of mine and he has made a special point of asking to be introduced to you. Lord Lamont. Miss Allen. There! Did I not do that well? Even your aunt would have approved of me, Jenny."

And with that she disappeared so suddenly that she might as well have been summoned, like a genie, by the rubbing of a lamp.

"Miss Carew is singularly obliging," Lord Lamont said with a smile. "I hope you do not mind."

"Oh, I am always willing to provide amusement," Jenny replied, her voice rich with ironic intonation. "It is a pity that my aunt is not at hand to amuse you, as well."

"Ah, ha!" he said. "So you have a sense of humor, Miss Allen. I thought as much the first time that I saw you, when you were talking to the distinguished doctor."

"My aunt puts her faith in him," Jenny said, tossing her head. No doubt Letty had told this gentleman that she came from the country and he thought she would know no better than to strike up a confidential conversation all at once. "That is all I have to know about his reputation."

"There is such a singular proof of loyalty in the face of reason as is quite suitable to this fair city," he replied. "You are most adaptable, Miss Allen. Why, I have known a deal of people who have managed to visit Bath a score of times without managing to adjust themselves to calling black white. I expect that, as a consequence, you will find Lady Madrigal's musical evenings memorable occasions."

Jenny bridled and bit her lip before making reply. "I cannot think, Sir," she declared, "what made you think that you could carp and criticize my aunt and her friends in front of me! I will make my own decision about Lady Madrigal's soirées and not depend on you to prejudice me in advance, if you please!"

"I see that I have made you angry, Miss Allen," he said. "And I am sorry for it. I am obliged to be caustic to dispel the ill humor into which this city always casts me. But that is no fit excuse perhaps."

Over his shoulder, Jenny saw her aunt, standing on tiptoe and striking her nose with her fan in such a distracted manner that she threatened to do herself an injury.

"I should think that if you do not like this place you ought to leave it," Jenny declared. "And now, you must excuse me, Sir. My aunt is waiting for me to join her, and I think I will prefer her company to yours."

And with burning cheeks she hurried away, but not before she saw that same mocking glint in his dark eyes.

chapter four

"*I will not pretend that it is not singularly provoking that Lady Carew has set her daughter on you, my dear,*" Lady Blunder said the next morning when they were sitting in the breakfast room, having just finished their tea and biscuits while Chow-chow, a singularly pampered lap dog of questionable pedigree, sat patiently waiting for scraps. "It puts me in an awkward situation. I would rather that you did not number the girl among your acquaintances, my dear, but I know your uncle will not agree."

Although Lady Blunder did not attend the Pump Room in dishabille and frowned on those who did, she was unassuming enough about the house to come down to breakfast in a dressing gown and cap which caused her to look so careworn that Jenny felt a twinge of conscience. Or perhaps it was not so much conscience as a general discomfort which had been with her ever since she had parted so sharply with Lord Lamont the evening before. Perhaps, she thought, Bath was not the place for her to be. Or perhaps she must learn to laugh at it as he did and have done taking anything, including her aunt's worries, seriously. She was here because she had nowhere else to go and because it was necessary that she marry. And if she took it seriously she must of needs feel trapped, while if she took it lightly it could be endured. No, more than endured. Enjoyed.

"You do not have to worry, Aunt," she said now, as a consequence. "I will pick up no bad habits from her. Come, smile a little. Only consider. The evening was a success."

Lady Blunder was forced to admit that that was true. "You cannot think how worried I was when we were separated," she said. "My dear, I was quite distracted, and I blame Lady Carew for it. But that is another matter, I suppose."

"Besides," Jenny reminded her. "You saw me soon enough with Mr. Basset."

"La, I was that relieved!" her aunt exclaimed. "What an excellent choice you made, my dear. Anyone who saw you must have realized that you have my taste, for he is well known to be a great wit."

"I saw that at once, Aunt," Jenny remarked, keeping her composure with some difficulty.

"I meet him often at Lady Madrigal's," Lady

Blunder went on. "I declare that when he plays the castanets it sends a tingle up my spine."

The thought of the Honorable Tommy Basset, whom she had last seen shifting from one foot to another in an agony of embarrassment, performing on the castanets with Latin abandon struck Jenny as so near an impossibility that she determined to withhold opinion on his musical ability until she had the pleasure of hearing him. Yes, that was the tone she must strike with herself. Lady Madrigal's musical evenings might include every sort of folly, not to mention nonsense, but why should she play the judge? If her aunt said that Mr. Basset was witty, then he should be, and, if she thrilled to his clappings, that was how it should be.

"And then I was so pleased when Sir Timity made such a point of occupying your attention," Lady Blunder went on, quite cheerful now. "He is an extraordinary dancer, is he not?"

"Extraordinary," Jenny assured her, remembering the absurd manner in which the gentleman in question had capered around the floor like a scarecrow gone mad.

"And certainly it was an honor to have a viscount take you to supper," her aunt declared, beaming at the memory of that triumph. "Lord Russell is a most important man and a widower to boot. There is nothing wrong with an older husband, my dear. They are always steady, and that counts for something, I like to think. And if you cannot love them in one way, you can be fond of them in another."

Jenny was aware of a sinking feeling. Apparently, no matter how she tried, she would not be able to take all this as lightly as she would like. Of course, it was only natural for her aunt to speak of marriage. No doubt as time went on she would do so increasingly. A good alliance. That was, no doubt, the way she would refer to it. And to think that she should actually think that Jenny could make a match with someone like Lord Russell, who was as corpulent as a man could be and still stay on his feet and who, if he could be believed, was suffering from such a case of gout as to make his days an agony and the nights only endurable by a lavish consumption of claret! Just to remember sitting beside him while he gobbled up his food with fewer manners than a common laborer made her feel cold inside. She remembered what efforts she had taken not to look around the room for fear that Lord Lamont might be watching her with that mocking smile.

As though there had been some sort of mental transference, her aunt chose that moment to utter Lord Lamont's name.

"How fortunate that I happened on you at that precise moment, my dear," she said, feeding Chow-chow a bit of biscuit spread with jam. "It would not have done for you to have been seen talking to him for long. Oh, dear, no! It would not have done indeed!"

"Certainly he is not the son of an ironmonger," Jenny replied with a good spirit which she was very far from feeling. Still, if she seemed to tease, her aunt might dismiss the subject.

"In matter of fact," her aunt said grimly, "he is a marquess, which, under ordinary circumstances, would make him more than eligible, of course. But he is to be avoided at all costs."

Much as she did not want to discuss Lord Lamont, Jenny's curiosity could not help but be aroused. "Is he so very dangerous then?" she asked in a low voice.

Lady Blunder arched her nose or seemed to, which was all very much the same thing, and her eyes stared more myopically than usual. "He has made his mother's life a misery," she declared. *"That* is all! Made her life a misery!"

And before Jenny could inquire how, Lady Blunder was telling her story with such enthusiasm that Chow-chow, sensing the precise moment when disipline might be expected to be relaxed, jumped to her voluminous lap and began to devour the remains of the biscuit from the plate.

"Lady Lamont is an intimate of mine, and so I know that there is no mistake," Lady Blunder went on. "The family estate is in Somerset—or perhaps in Kent. I cannot remember which. No matter. She prefers to live in Bath on account of her health, which is, at best, precarious. She suffers a good deal of dropsy and a number of other complaints. You will remember that when

Dr. Dangle came here yesterday at four he was speaking of one of his patients whom he had just retrieved from death's door. Well, that was Lady Lamont!"

The case against the son was not immediately made clear, for Jenny gathered that he had come to Bath on his mother's account in response to a letter from Dr. Dangle informing him that she was dying. Jenny remembered the expression in his eyes as he watched the physician make his irregular way across the Pump Room the morning before and thought she might have found an answer for Lord Lamont's cynicism in that regard at least. Indeed, if Dr. Dangle was nursing his mother, it was a mercy that she was still alive. Having observed the doctor for a second time the day before, Jenny was convinced that it was only due to the extraordinary soundness of her aunt's constitution that she had not been made a permanent invalid years ago as a result of his curious treatment.

"The thing is," Lady Blunder went on, "that Oliver will not take her seriously. That is to say, he will persist in saying that she is quite well and only feels off color because of the combination of the waters and Dr. Dangle's pills."

Jenny's opinion of the young marquess underwent a slight modification at her aunt's words. Not that she intended ever to excuse him for the way he had mocked her! No, indeed! But at least it was easier now to understand his cynical approach to Bath. Indeed, her aunt's next words did not surprise her.

"He mocks at everything," Lady Blunder said. "Young ladies will flock after him whenever his mother's health recalls him from managing his estate. But he will take nothing seriously, and his mother has quite despaired of seeing him married. His values are all askew. That is the thing of it. I cannot tell you how much it hurts his dear mother. Of course, he is personable enough. If I had not appeared as I did, no doubt you would have been taken in. Now that you know the truth about his character, you can make a point of avoiding him in future. His mother is quite a different matter, of course. We will pay her a visit tomorrow since she is far too ill to come to the Pump Room and must have the water brought to her, I understand."

"I do not think..." Jenny began, determined not to go.

"No need to fear an encounter with the son," Lady Lamont assured her. "I would not allow it. If we go at ten we can be certain he will be riding on the downs. His mother tells me that he likes to think the city suffocates him. But of course that is simply something he says because he knows she does not like to hear it. Chow-chow! Whatever are you doing! Get down at once!" And then, turning her attention back to Jenny: "You understand now, my dear, that he is a thoroughly bad fellow and to be avoided at all costs!"

"Whose character are you defaming now, Tabitha?" Sir Simon demanded in his usual languid way. "Really, I think I must protest. You will have the poor child believing that Bath is alive with ruffians and scoundrels, not to mention murderers and footpads and every other sort of miscreant."

Jenny was glad to see him, for he always brought with him a lightness of touch to relieve the general air of catastrophe with which his sister liked to surround herself. Indeed, she could well understand why Letty's mother found him so attractive. Jenny smiled at him as he came into the breakfast room, a tall, imposing gentleman even without his wig, with the long skirts of his brocade dressing gown trailing on the floor.

"I was warning her of Oliver," Lady Blunder announced. "Dear Devina's son. The one who treats her so miserably."

Sir Simon helped himself to an apple from the bowl on the table. "Well, as for that," he announced blandly, "the woman is either a fool or a hypochondriac or both. I never have decided. What would you have him do, I wonder? Sit about here and comfort her for allowing that idiot Dangle to systematically ruin her health? How many times has she had word sent to him that she was dying? How many times has he had to drop his business and make the trip here?

I wonder he bothers to come at all now that she has cried wolf so many times."

"Your uncle prides himself in contradicting me in everything!" Lady Blunder exclaimed, pushing her chair back from the table in the manner of someone about to make direct attack. When she rose she and Sir Simon stared at one another in silence for a moment, giving Jenny the benefit of a fine view of their craggy profiles. Then, bending to scoop up Chow-chow, Lady Blunder bustled from the room.

"I am afraid I am a grave disappointment to your aunt, my dear," Sir Simon said with a laugh. "She would like it better if I would always agree. But she gets bees in her bonnet, you understand, and once she has formed an opinion she will not change it, no matter how much evidence there is that she should. Young Lord Lamont is a case in point. Why, he's a brilliant fellow who..."

"Would you mind awfully if we did not talk about him?" Jenny murmured.

Her uncle took another bite from the apple and eyed her quizzically. "That's a strange thing to say," he muttered. "He's the sort of fellow I want you to get to know."

"I know him already, I'm afraid," Jenny said, coolly, drinking tea which had long since gone cold. "At least we were introduced by Letty."

Sir Simon beamed. "Ah, Letty!" he exclaimed. "She takes after her mother, the little chit. Tell me, what did you think of her, my dear?"

Jenny indicated that she liked her very much indeed and amused her uncle by telling of the way Letty had prevailed on Sir Roger Ramsdale and the Honorable Tommy Basset to dance with them.

"Now that's the sort of gentleman your aunt will try to pawn off on you," Sir Simon declared. "I know them both, to my misfortune, for I am certain they must be two of the dullest chaps that I have ever met. One of them plays the castanets, I believe. Tabitha says he is a musical genius, and I dread to think what that may mean."

"No doubt I will hear him tonight at Lady Madrigal's," Jenny replied. "I will make a close evaluation, Uncle, especially for you."

"Ah, you're a good girl, Jenny," Sir Simon said, twirling one of the black curls which had escaped the mob cap around his finger. "And you must be careful that you are not too much that way. Simply because your aunt wants to attend one of Lady Madrigal's evenings does not mean you have to go, you know. I had meant to play a few hands of whist at Wiltshire's, but if you like we could go to the subscription concert. It would give you your excuse at any rate."

Jenny assured her uncle that he was very kind but that she would be her aunt's companion for the night. "She feels that I am a grave responsibility," she told him, "and I want to prove to her that I do not mean to be a burden. In which case I must be with her for a time to demonstrate that she can depend on my common sense."

Sir Simon smiled. "An admirable ambition, my dear," he said. "The only problem that I can see is that if you *are* sensible—and I have no doubts in that quarter—then you will soon see that she is not. In a word, if you are to win her approval you may be asked to do some very silly things indeed. Like taking refreshment with Lord Russell. That was *her* doing, I suppose. I must confess it made me angry at the time. Still, I do not mean to interfere with my opinions, child."

Jenny felt a strange and sudden sadness for what reason she did not know. Perhaps it was because it was so clear her uncle wanted nothing but her happiness.

"You'll come to me if I can help you?" he asked in a low voice.

Jenny told him that she would and left the room abruptly so that he would not see the tears which came from nowhere to sting her eyes.

chapter five

Lady Madrigal's fine town house was located in
Saw Close, quite near the house where Bath's
famous Master of Ceremonies, Beau Nash, had
lived until his death twenty years ago, or so
Lady Blunder assured Jenny as they descended
from their carriage.

"He was before my time, of course," she declared as they mounted the steps to the gracious
brick building. But he put an end to dueling
and did all manner of other things to raise the
general tone of the city. I will say more on the
subject later. You should learn the history of
Bath, but this is not the time. Prepare yourself
for an evening of sheer enjoyment, my dear. And
I assure you that you will meet no one here
except the *crème de la crème!*"

Half an hour later, Jenny was reduced to

shifting restlessly in her chair, and an hour after that she had all that she could do to keep from yawning behind her hand. Never in her life had she hoped to hear such a mishmash of musical presentations by so many unabashed amateurs.

The evening had begun with a ballad of her own composing delivered by a baleful lady who sang of love and shepherds and larks rising on the downs while staring at the audience seated on gilt chairs in the main salon with such a malignant expression that everyone appeared to be quite cowed. Whatever the lady's experience with bucolic passion had been, it clearly had been far from pleasant despite the verses which she mouthed.

Next had come a young lady who had performed on the harpsichord quite wildly and with such a fine disregard for beat or harmony as to make Jenny clench her teeth. "Lovely," Lady Blunder kept murmuring. "Quite, quite the loveliest thing I have ever heard."

Lady Madrigal herself announced the performers, extolling them all in such a lavish manner that, at first, despite previous disappointments, Jenny's hopes were raised repeatedly, only to come crashing down apace.

Perhaps the most appalling rendition of a piece of music was accomplished by a gentleman who played the viola with such a dreadful twanging of the strings that Jenny was amazed the hostess could keep such a self-satisfied smile

52

on her lips. When the piece was finally brought to an end, Jenny could scárcely believe her eyes to see several members of the company leap to their feet and cry out "Bravo!"

But it was two of her acquaintances who provided the *pièce de résistance* of the evening. Jenny had not imagined that a lute and castanets could be combined to produce any music outside of Bedlam, but Sir Timity and the Honorable Tommy Basset managed it, the former strolling among the company like an emaciated minstrel in a completely unself-conscious sort of way which made Jenny turn hot and cold from sheer embarrassment, while young Mr. Basset, losing all inhibitions, despite the shyness he had exhibited to her the night before, danced and pranced and whirled about and shook the castanets with all his might.

After this Lady Madrigal herself entertained the company with an aria from Gluck's *Alceste* which seemed to go on forever. It was at this stage that Jenny had had to fight to keep from yawning, and she was excessively relieved when, at the conclusion of the piece, Lady Madrigal announced that tea would be served directly.

Feeling that hypocrisy could be carried only so far and that she had expended her small store in the simple matter of her applause, Jenny did not accompany her aunt, who bustled off to congratulate all the performers in turn. Rising from her chair to stretch her stiffened limbs,

Jenny was startled to hear her name spoken and, turning, found herself looking straight into the dark eyes of Lord Lamont himself.

"But what are you doing here!" she exclaimed before she could think of anything except the sheer surprise of seeing him.

"My mother desired to hear the music," he said simply, "and requested my company. Nothing else would have made me volunteer to suffer so, I assure you."

"But your mother is on her death bed, Sir!" Jenny declared. "At least that was why you came to Bath, or so my aunt told me."

Only then did she pause to think that she was being too natural by far to someone she had dismissed in such a brusque manner the evening before. Perhaps she had forgotten to be hostile because the mocking smile had left his lips, although clearly he was still amused. In matter of fact he laughed when Jenny mentioned his mother's death bed.

"My mother approaches and retreats from death with such rapidity that I am certain that Charon, if he exists, has quite given up expecting a fare from her. In fact her recuperation often finds her so vigorous that I am soon forced to retreat to the country to rest myself from so much exertion."

All this was said in such a dry voice that Jenny did not know how much she could believe. If he were the wicked son her aunt had painted, why had he submitted to what he must have

54

known would be a boring evening of such stunning proportions? And why, if he knew his mother was never in the deathly condition that she claimed, did he come to Bath when it was clear that he found nothing here to admire?

"You do not believe in your mother's illnesses then, Sir?" Jenny asked him, and when he made no reply she saw that he had been distracted apparently by the sight of their reflection in a large gilt-edged mirror hanging on the wall opposite. Most of the company had retreated to the room where tea was being served, and they had a clear view of themselves, the slender girl in her polonaise of violet silk with an overskirt of deeper lavender and the gentleman with the haunting eyes in evening dress of dark blue satin with only a touch of white lawn at the throat and sleeves to break the pattern.

"I think we make a handsome couple, Miss Allen," Lord Lamont murmured. "A perfect advertisement for this city where appearances are all and substance nothing."

She knew that he was mocking her again, but she let it pass and asked her question over again. Lord Lamont considered for a minute.

"If, by that, you mean to ask me if I have faith in Dr. Dangle's diagnosis," he replied, "the answer is clearly no."

Jenny pursed her lips. "In that case, why do you not insist that she see another physician?"

"Insist, Miss Allen?" He laughed. "It is quite clear that you have never met my mother. I assure you that she takes my advice about nothing."

"But if you actually think that Dr. Dangle is doing her some harm..."

"You are persistent, Miss Allen," he interrupted her. "Meet my mother first and then we will continue this discussion. In the meantime, you have asked your question and now I claim the right to ask one of my own. Do you find Bath agreeable?"

Jenny had the strange feeling that she was being tested and yet that was absurd. Lord Lamont was making idle conversation with her. She knew his opinion of the city, and she could either agree or not.

"There is a great deal of artifice about," she said after a pause. "People pretend that things are as they want them to be and not as they really are. And some of the customs are strange."

"Like this evening's entertainment?" he asked her.

"Yes. I suppose that is the sort of thing I mean," Jenny said earnestly. "And yet, on the whole, I find it all harmless enough, and no doubt some parts of it will prove entertaining."

"No doubt," he said, but something in his face and eyes seemed to close. It was a curious impression to receive, but Jenny felt as though she had been shut out. No doubt she had failed his test. And what of that! Did he think she was about to let him form her opinions for her? What arrogance! No doubt her aunt had been quite right in her evaluation of him.

She meant to leave him, but at that moment Sir Timity appeared to present her with a cup of tea. "Sir," he said, bowing to Lord Lamont, whom he appeared to know. "Miss Allen. Allow me to provide you with some refreshment. I saw that you were being detained here. Or, rather, your aunt took notice of it and asked me to...well, to bring you some tea."

"Be frank and tell Miss Allen straight out that her aunt wanted you to interrupt in the hopes that I might go away," Lord Lamont said in his old mocking way.

Sir Timity's shoulders were so insubstantial that when he shrugged them, as he did now, it was scarcely noticeable. "I assure you that I have been yearning to ask Miss Allen what she thought of the duet I played with Mr. Basset," he replied. "I am not one to boast, but I thought it a thrilling performance."

"And unusual," Lord Lamont said dryly. "I do not believe I have ever heard the lute and castanets in combination before."

It was all politely said, but Jenny knew that behind the words lay the implication that he would not greatly care if he never heard those particular instruments in duet again. And she agreed! But what could she do but lie, with Sir Timity looking at her so hopefully? Indeed, when she saw that they were about to be joined by the Honorable Tommy Basset, she knew that she must give up all thoughts of honesty. Now that he was no longer making an abandoned performance, Mr. Basset had become his usual shy self, and it was clear from the hesitation of his approach and his downcast eyes that he was suffering agonies of timidity.

"Both of you are to be congratulated," Jenny declared firmly. "An enchanting performance. Unusual, as Lord Lamont says, but enchanting, all the same."

She *would* not let him catch her eyes. Instead she turned her attention strictly to the two performers, who made it clear from their response that they could not get enough of congratulation.

"And Lady Madrigal has such a...such a powerful voice," Jenny said in desperation, trying to turn the conversation a little before she ran out of adjectives to pertain to them.

"She could make her fortune if she went upon the stage to do an opera in London," Sir Timity declared in a decided way, excusing himself long enough to rescue one of his white silk stockings which had managed to detach itself from his pantaloons and was sliding down his skinny shank.

Since Lady Madrigal on a London stage was clearly inconceivable, Jenny could make no answer and merely smiled and nodded as Sir Timity lavished high praise on all the other performers and ended by declaring that Lady Madrigal's evenings raised the cultural level of

Bath to that of London and sometimes, he thought, beyond. Jenny did not dare to even glance at Lord Lamont at this point and was glad enough to be interrupted by her aunt, who was in the company of a languid-appearing lady who was leaning on her arm in the way of someone who does not have the strength to make her way by herself. In spite of this, she appeared in every other way to be in the full flush of health if skin and eyes were any indication. Otherwise, she was a little woman whose carefully coiffured hair was fine as silk.

"My mother approaches," Jenny heard Lord Lamont murmur. "Appearances will deceive you but, believe me, she has a will of iron."

Lady Blunder's eyes made it clear that she was not at all pleased that Jenny had remained so long in Lord Lamont's company, but clearly, with his mother in attendance, there was nothing she could say. Introductions were performed all around, and Lady Lamont was helped, at her request, into a chair.

"Too exhausting," she declared weakly, pressing the back of one hand against her forehead and closing her eyes. "Look in my reticule, dear Tabitha, and see if you can find my vinaigrette. Perhaps a whiff will restore me."

"You should not have come out tonight, Devina," Lady Blunder said, staring at Lord Lamont angrily, as she rummaged in his mother's reticule. "Really, I wonder that your son permitted it."

"I made the effort for Oliver's sake," Lady Lamont murmured. "I thought that if I could keep up the pretense of recovery, he would feel free to leave Bath without any sense of guilt."

"You always were an unselfish mother," Lady Blunder declared, holding the restorative under her friend's nose. "I have said it before and I will say it again, you are much too good for him."

"Really, Tabitha," Lady Lamont protested, opening her eyes. "You are too hard on Oliver. It is tiresome for him to constantly be summoned from the country to my sick bed. Ah, well, the dear doctor believes that my next relapse will be my last so there will soon be no more dashing down to Bath for Oliver. There. I believe I am feeling a bit better. These attacks come and go constantly, you know."

"I cannot allow you to make the effort yet," Lady Blunder replied. "Stay seated at least until the color comes back to your cheeks, Devina."

Since Lady Lamont's complexion was, if anything, a little high, Jenny wondered at this but said nothing. She had the uncomfortable feeling that the gentleman beside her had been more put upon than her aunt had indicated. Of course, it might be that appearances were deceptive, and certainly the lady's manner was listless enough. But there was something carping about her tone, and certainly it could not be pleasant for Lord Lamont to hear her discuss private affairs quite so openly.

"I am afraid that I do not have the energy to address myself to your niece, Tabitha," Lady Lamont was saying now. "You know how it exhausts me to meet new people. But of course I want to know her because of the affection which I feel for you, my dear, if for no other reason. Come to me tomorrow when I shall have had my rest."

"But, of course, we will," Lady Blunder assured her friend. "If it is convenient for you to receive us at ten, that is. Any other hour would be impossible, I am afraid, as long as your son is staying with you."

This remark was made to the accompaniment of such a significant glance in Lord Lamont's direction as to make Jenny flush with embarrassment. What possessed her aunt to make her dislike of the young marquess so clear? She was ready to accept everything Lady Blunder had told her, she supposed, but such rudeness was uncalled for, surely. She glanced at him to find his handsome face expressionless.

"Well, well, I must be off," Lady Lamont said wearily. "I hope you enjoyed the evening, Oliver. It is the least that I can do to make certain that you have some entertainment. No matter how much it costs me. Oh dear, I believe that I will need Dr. Dangle early in the morning."

And off she went, clinging to her son's arm as though she meant to collapse at any moment, leaving Jenny to remember the look in Lord Lamont's dark eyes as they had parted, a look which seemed to say that he was as alien to her as he was to the rest of the company.

"Well, now!" Lady Blunder exclaimed when they were gone. "You have seen at first hand precisely what I mean. He is arrogant! He condescends! He attends to his mother, but grudgingly! Have a care, my girl, and keep out of his way. He has broken too many hearts before now for me to want you to risk yours as well."

Jenny tossed her black curls and turned to where Sir Timity stood in close conversation with young Mr. Basset. "Nothing could be less likely, Aunt," she said with warmth. "You may rest assured that I will never risk anything with Lord Lamont, let alone my heart."

chapter six

As though the evening had not been long and tiresome enough, Jenny and her aunt returned home to the terrace house on the Circus to find the household in turmoil with candles lit in every room and servants scurrying about and other signs of general consternation.

"It is the master, Your Ladyship," Grout, the footman, explained. "It seems that he was set upon by footpads as he was coming from the square and was knocked quite senseless by a blow to the head."

"Oh dear! Oh dear!" Lady Blunder exclaimed. "Dr. Dangle must be called immediately!"

"I took the liberty of sending for him," the footman replied. "And a general search was instigated once it was found that he was not in his quarters. I would have sent for someone else, particularly when it was discovered that he was in a certain condition, but I know how particular you are about him and, as a consequence..."

But Lady Blunder did not linger. She set off at once to bustle up the stairs, leaving Jenny to inquire what condition it was that Grout referred to.

"Well, Miss, I do not think that he is much worse than usual," was the indirect reply she received.

And, indeed, when Jenny reached her uncle's bedroom, she saw that Dr. Dangle seemed to be in much the same disposition she had seen him in that morning at the Pump Room. Sir Simon lay upon the bed with his eyes closed and a face which was so pale that she found she was relieved to see that he was breathing. Dr. Dangle, who had laid aside both his coat and his periwig, was bending over the patient in his shirt-sleeves. Lady Blunder was standing just inside the door, stuffing a handkerchief in her mouth, presumably to keep herself from screaming.

"No need to worry," Dr. Dangle declared with a considerable slur to his words. "I'll have him right as rain after the operation."

"What operation?" Jenny demanded, hurrying to the bedside, where she could see a bump the size of an egg high on her uncle's temple.

The doctor groped about for his coat which was hanging on a chair and delved into a pocket from which he drew out some dirty dressings and several instruments made all the more ominous by signs of rust.

"Fetch some water," he said to Jenny, no doubt mistaking her for a servant. "Hot or cold, it makes no difference."

"I do not intend to leave this room, Sir, until you put away those instruments!" Jenny declared. "My uncle has a swelling on his head. He may have a concussion. But he is in no need of an operation even if your hands were steady enough to perform one."

Lady Blunder appeared to say something but, since her handkerchief was still stuffed in her mouth, it was impossible to make any sense of it.

Dr. Dangle assumed a dignified posture, marred only by his inability to stand without swaying. "I am the doctor here," he said as though to reassure himself that it was really so. "I mean to perform—I mean to perform a trepan of this—of this gentleman's cranium."

"You will do no such thing, sir!" Jenny exclaimed. "I will not allow it! My uncle needs to have a poultice applied to his head. That is the first thing."

The doctor did not appear to notice that he had been interrupted. Indeed, he seemed to be concentrating on focusing his eyes.

"Any blood that might be extravasated either above or below the dura mater..." he droned, selecting one instrument from his collection and bending over the figure on the bed.

Jenny reached out her hand to prevent him from doing whatever it was that had occurred to his muddled mind. In the background her aunt, having apparently unplugged her mouth, began to wail. Simultaneously Sir Simon opened his eyes and, seeing Dr. Dangle apparently prepared to make an incision in his head, gave a great cry and leaped out of the bed. At the same moment Lady Carew's voice was heard in the hall, and, as Sir Simon dashed from the bed chamber, she dashed into it and they collided in what might, under other circumstances, have been a fond embrace.

Matters settled themselves eventually. Dr. Dangle was dismissed over Lady Blunder's protests. Sir Simon was convinced to return to bed. Lady Carew insisted on preparing a poultice with the help of Cook, and Jenny, after seeing her aunt settled in the sitting room with a glass of ratafia, discovered Letty in the corridor.

"Mama and I were just coming from the concert when we heard the news," she explained to Jenny as they made their way upstairs. "We came at once to give assistance, and I was somehow overlooked in the excitement."

Having assured herself that Lady Carew wanted no assistance in her role as nurse, Jenny led her friend to her own bed chamber where they settled down together on the window seat, looking down over the city where the lights still twinkled in the public gardens by the river.

"What a nuisance this has been for you,"

Letty murmured, taking Jenny's hand. "Tell me all about it, do. It will make you feel all the better to talk it out."

Strangely enough, Jenny found that this was true. Beginning with the account of finding Dr. Dangle about to operate on her uncle, she found herself backtracking to the evening's entertainment at Lady Madrigal's.

"What a strange introduction you have had to Bath," Letty said when she was through. "Last night at the assembly ball I saw you with Lord Russell. You cannot allow your aunt to choose your company, you know. As Mama says, she does not discriminate."

This comment threw Jenny into a fit of laughter which did not rise so much from amusement as from the irony of things. Her aunt put such great emphasis on discrimination, yet Jenny was well aware by now that just the opposite was true.

"Take Lord Lamont as an example," Letty exclaimed, eager to make her case. "I introduced you to him at the assembly ball...."

"Because he asked you to?" Jenny inquired.

"Why, as for that, I did not give him the opportunity," Letty said blithely. "I wanted something a good deal better than Mr. Basset for you and so I..."

"My aunt would have it that he makes a business of breaking hearts," Jenny murmured. "And I am not speaking of Mr. Basset."

For the first time Letty appeared flustered.

"It is not Lord Lamont's fault, surely, if women tend to throw themselves upon him. And because he has an ironic turn of mind and does not think highly of Bath society..."

"He leads them on and means nothing of it?"

"That is not what I meant to say at all," Letty declared impatiently. "Still, I do not blame you for being prickly, given the evening you have spent. He finds it amusing to observe, I think, but he does not wish to be a part of what goes on here. And if ladies will rush after him, he cannot help it. Certainly I have never seen him encourage any one of them. But they *will* fasten their affections and then he will go away. I suppose there has been a certain pattern to it, but it is none of Lord Lamont's fault, I assure you. He must come here from time to time on his mother's account. They say he is more patient with her than she deserves."

"Whether he is patient or not I cannot be certain," Jenny replied, "although my aunt has expressed a positive opinion that he is not. But from what I observed of the lady tonight..."

"You did not tell me that you had met her!" Letty exclaimed. "What, and was Lord Lamont with her?"

Jenny had confined her account of the soirée at Lady Madrigal's to a description of the musical renditions, but now she admitted that Lord Lamont had been in reluctant attendance.

"And did he seek you out?" Letty demanded impatiently.

"We encountered one another," Jenny told her. "That was all."

"You sound as though it was not a matter of consequence," Letty said, almost accusingly. "You cannot think how many young ladies there are in Bath tonight who would have liked to be in your shoes."

"Anyone of them could have been for all I care," Jenny replied, "for he is interested in nothing except to demonstrate that I and all the rest are foolish and misguided in our ways."

And, remembering the praise she had lavished on Sir Timity and Mr. Basset, she blushed and changed the subject immediately.

"I think that we should see how my uncle is," she said. "And my aunt, as well."

"And are you glad that I am here to keep you from taking everything too seriously?" Letty demanded, rising. She had chosen to wear a rose-colored muslin gown to the concert, and, even in the light of a single candle, it served to make a satisfactory contrast with her thick red hair, which she had caught high with silver combs. Jenny envied her for appearing to be so self-assured and part of the social scene.

"You like your life then?" she said in a low voice. "You are quite satisfied with balls and concerts and all the rest?"

For a moment Letty's face seemed to darken, and then she threw back her head and laughed. "I like to enjoy myself," she said. "What is there wrong with that? Sooner or later, I suppose, I will marry and lead a more sober existence. But for the time things are well enough to suit me. Why do you ask?"

Jenny found that she was hard pressed to find an answer. Granted that, thanks to her aunt, she had met any number of peculiar people. But, as Letty had hinted, this could be remedied once she knew the society in which she found herself more intimately. And yet that was no real answer. Life was as unreal here as though it had been painted on a screen. And yet, at the very best, she could only adapt it to her best advantage. Find someone eligible whom she could admire. Not hope for more. Somehow it did not seem enough. And yet she knew that, given her situation, it was more than she had hoped for. To become a governess was her only other choice, and she knew enough of how they were treated to shy from that possibility.

"It doesn't matter," she said to Letty, taking up the candle and opening the door into the hall. "I only wondered if you were happy."

Her friend took her arm with sudden urgency and would have answered if Lady Blunder's voice had not been heard raised hysterically. The two girls hurried down the hall to find that she was mounting the stairs with Gertrude, looking most distressed, behind her.

"If my brother must have a nurse then it should be me!" she cried as she encountered Jenny on the landing. "Lady Carew has taken advantage of an opportunity to insinuate herself into this household and I...and I will not have it!"

No sooner had she finished her pronouncement than the door of her brother's bed chamber was flung open and Lady Carew emerged with Cook, who was carrying a large basin of water. Behind them Sir Simon could be seen resting on propped pillows, his head neatly bound in a white bandage.

"Sir Simon is resting comfortably now," Lady Carew announced so pleasantly that, if she had not known it was an impossibility, Jenny would have thought that she had not heard what her aunt had just said. "He is conscious and suffering no more than a slight headache. Cook means to fetch him a cup of tea. Other than that a little quiet....But then, of course, Lady Blunder, you must be the judge of what will be best for him."

Jenny's aunt huffed and puffed a little, but before she could go on Lady Carew had continued in her usual charming way. Although her hair was white, here in the candlelight she looked more youthful than her years and, indeed, quite lovely.

"Believe me, Lady Blunder, I would never have interfered had you not been so distracted. And, of course, that is to be expected considering that you are closer to your brother than anyone in the entire world."

Her words trickled out like syrup as she tripped down the stairs and put her hand on Lady Blunder's arm. "La, my dear," she said.

"When we are upset, we never know what we are saying. But I know you would not want your brother to be distressed. Go to him. Comfort him. No one else can take your place by his side at a time like this."

And off she went downstairs after giving Lady Blunder a little kiss. After a moment's consideration, while Lady Carew could be heard telling the footman that she and her daughter were leaving and that she would like her pelisse, Jenny's aunt continued up the stairs and went into her brother's room.

"Mother has taken her by surprise," Letty whispered to Jenny. "How very clever she is with people. Of course, she will never succeed completely with your aunt. But I think they could exist together in the same house. At least I hope for your aunt's sake that they can."

"Letty!" Lady Carew called from below.

"Do you really think my uncle will ask your mother to marry him?" Jenny replied in a low voice.

"If Mama has her way he will," Letty replied lightly. "Only think. Then we will be related, although I cannot think precisely how. Cousins, perhaps. Step-cousins! Is there such a thing, do you think?"

"Letty!" Lady Carew called again.

"And does she love him?" Jenny asked.

There were so many shadows on the landing that Jenny could not see her friend's expression clearly, but she spoke more earnestly than was her wont. "I do not think she knows what it is to love truly," Letty murmured. "But, oh, *I do* know, Jenny. That was what I meant to tell you when you asked if I was happy."

"Letty!" Lady Carew called again, and this time her voice, sweet as it was, was insistent.

"Yes, Mother," Letty called. And, in an aside to Jenny: "Next time we meet I will confide in you if you will let me. I *must* tell someone!"

And, pressing Jenny's hand in her own for a moment, she was gone. The door had closed behind her and her mother by the time Jenny had reached the hall, leaving Jenny to wonder what new complication in her life Letty's secret would bring.

chapter seven

Morning found Sir Simon completely recovered,
or so he insisted. Appearing downstairs in his
elegant dressing gown, he gave little sign of the
injury he had suffered, having removed his
bandage and assured himself that the lump had
substantially subsided.

"If you ever again allow Dr. Dangle within
two feet of me, Tabitha," he warned her as he
drank his morning tea, "I will not be responsible. I find the thought that you might have
stood by and let him operate on me so appalling
that it does not do me any good to think about
it. But I will strangle the man with these two
hands if he ever tries to lay a hand on me again,
damme if I won't."

All of this was said with a good deal more
warmth than Sir Simon was accustomed to

showing, and, no doubt as a consequence, Lady Blunder made no attempt to argue with him. Instead she made a great to-do about buttering him a biscuit and said that on no account was he to stir outside the house today.

However, that was far from her own intention, as Jenny soon discovered, for promptly at half past eight the sedan chairs were waiting outside. So intent was Lady Blunder in reaching the Pump Room to spread the news of what had happened to her brother to anyone who might not have heard, that she did not protest too much when Jenny announced that, since it was such a pleasant day, she intended to walk.

"Be careful not to fall, my dear!" Lady Blunder called out the window of her box as she was being carried away by the four puffing chairmen. "Gay Street is so very steep."

There were other warnings but she had soon been carried so far away that Jenny could not hear them. She only knew that they were being spoken by virtue of seeing her aunt's mouth move as she leaned farther and farther out the window, as though a continent was about to separate them rather than the side of a hill.

It was strange, Jenny thought, as she made her way along the cobbled street, which spread here, at the Circus, into a circle, what a difference a few days had made in her life. With the elderly cousin in Yorkshire she had had very little excitement, indeed. Even visitors were few and far between. And before that, when her father and mother were living, life in a village vicarage had been very quiet, too. She had seen her life opening out when she had been told that she was to go to Bath. She had heard stories of the famous spa. She had thought life would be a constant whirl. And so it was. And yet the freedom she had speculated about was nowhere to be seen, except perhaps for Letty. Her aunt and uncle chose the rules each preferred to govern their existence. Dr. Dangle had his role and Lady Madrigal had another. Yes, that was it. That was what she knew was required of her. A role. She could not be the innocent up from the country for long. And what must be determined now was who it was that she should be.

But the morning air was balmy, and the sun sparkled on the rooftops and the river sliding by below. And Gay Street was already beginning to be crowded with sedan chairs and carts and carriages of all varieties. As Jenny approached the Pump Room there was more and more bustle in the air, and she gave herself over to it with relief. Bath was a seductress, she decided, who could arrange, if you would let her, to give you no time at all to consider anything, least of all who it was you were to be.

The Pump Room was as crowded as usual, and there was the customary informal quality of clothing which so offended Lady Blunder. Jenny had no difficulty in finding her aunt, despite the press, since she was the center of a group of ladies and gentlemen who, having apparently finished listening to her story, were voicing their opinions excitedly.

"Such a thing never would have happened when Beau Nash ran this city!" Lady Madrigal announced in a penetrating voice, regardless of the near certainty that the present Master of Ceremonies was somewhere in the room. "Footpads, indeed! I do not know what Bath is coming to!"

"It is bad enough to have one's purse taken, but it adds insult to injury to be beaten on the head as well!" Sir Timity declared.

The Honorable Tommy Basset diffidently suggested that it was a "demmed" shame, and Lady Blunder went on to retell her story to a new group of friends who had been attracted by the excitement.

All in all it was quite an hour before Lady Blunder was ready to leave, and she chided herself for having lost track of the time, pausing to interrupt herself from time to time by glancing over her shoulder at those she left behind and making farewell gestures with her fan as though she could not bear to tear herself away.

"You will recall that we are to visit Lady Lamont at ten," she said to Jenny as they emerged into the courtyard before the Abbey. "Dear Devina is very punctual herself and expects others to be the same."

Jenny wanted to protest, but she suspected that it would do no good. Besides, what could be more natural than that her aunt should want her friends to come to know her niece? It was selfish, she told herself, to shy away from Lady Lamont simply because she was sick or sorry for herself or both. Would she have felt the same reluctance to make the visit, she wondered, if she had known that, instead of out riding on the downs, Lord Lamont would be at the house? The last thought made her angry with herself, and she followed her aunt without comment.

Lady Lamont resided in a house which faced the North Parade. Indeed, since it was the end house of the row, her drawing room windows looked straight down onto the river. Altogether her accommodations were charming, and it was apparent to Jenny, although she did not say so, that, however poor a son Lord Lamont might be, he made more than ample financial provision for his mother. It was at the moment that this thought came into her mind that the gentleman himself made an appearance, dressed for riding in a dark blue jacket, calf-colored trousers and Hessian boots.

"But you are supposed to be away at this hour, Sir!" Lady Blunder exclaimed.

Lord Lamont bowed, but not before Jenny had seen the sardonic expression in his eyes. Rising from the settee, where she and her aunt had been waiting to be summoned to his mother's bedside, she went to one of the broad windows and looked down at the swirling waters of the Avon.

"As you see, Madam," she heard him say, "I am on my way. Dr. Dangle is still with my mother, as you must have been told, but he will be leaving shortly. In fact, here he is."

Jenny turned in time to see her aunt quite literally crouch before the little man who came stumbling into the room. Indeed, she went to the extreme of clasping her hands beneath her chin in an attitude of supplication, which did not match at all her usual rather haughty demeanor.

"Dear Dr. Dangle!" she cried. "I cannot tell you how very sorry I am about the events of last night. My niece is short tempered. Besides, she was perturbed. She did not know what she was saying! Come, Jenny, and tell the doctor in your own words."

Jenny made a quick consideration, while Dr. Dangle stared at her aunt in a befuddled sort of way. He looked as though he had had even more difficulty than usual this morning in making his toilette. Indeed, he had forgotten his cravat, and it appeared that his shoes did not match for one sported a large buckle and the other was quite bare.

"I am truly sorry, Aunt," Jenny said in a low voice, "but I cannot, in all honesty, take back a word I said. Because I meant them all. Yes, every one! And I would say the same if it should ever happen again!"

"I think you are talking in an addled way, Madam," the doctor said, pausing to hiccup discretely behind one dirty hand. "Some distemper or other, I fancy. Here is a bottle of salts. Three doses daily. The fee will be one guinea."

"You must allow my niece to make amends for having insulted you," Lady Blunder insisted.

"Insulted me, dear lady? Whatever do you mean?" And he wove an uncertain path around the settee on which Lady Blunder was half crouched, half seated, winking broadly at Jenny as he passed her as though she were a wench on a street corner.

"Last night," Lady Blunder persisted. "When you came to our house to treat my brother."

"To treat your brother," Dr. Dangle said reflectively, pausing in his uncertain stroll about the room. Jenny did not want to look at Lord Lamont, so certain was she of the expression he must be wearing. How it must amuse him to see her aunt make a fool of herself in this manner.

"You meant to operate," Lady Blunder insisted.

"Good God! Did I indeed!" the physician exclaimed. "It is a very good thing your niece stopped me, damme if it ain't. Well, well! Your mother is very poorly, Your Lordship. The effort of attending last night's entertainment, I believe. I have left her the necessary medicines, and she is to remain in bed for today, at least. If I were you..."

"Yes," Lord Lamont said evenly. "If you were me?"

Dr. Dangle clutched his head, muttered something indistinct about a migrim and had half pulled a bottle of medicine from his pocket when, realizing that he was observed, he lurched out of the room, nearly knocking over a female servant who was about to enter.

"Her Ladyship sends word that she is too ill to see your niece today, Lady Blunder," the servant said, keeping her face expressionless, as well-trained menials always should. "However, she is most desirous of speaking to you about an important matter."

Lady Blunder hunched her shoulders and her nose simultaneously, leaving no doubt in the mind of anyone that she was reluctant to leave Jenny alone with her old friend's son.

"No need to worry, Lady Blunder," Lord Lamont said dryly. "I am on my way."

"Wait!" Jenny said as he turned to leave the room. "Unless you *must* go, I would like to have a word with you, Sir."

Lady Blunder frowned until her myopic eyes nearly met, but there was very little else that she could do. She could not make a fuss before one of the servants. Jenny could see her mind switching from one possibility to another. No, she could not order Lord Lamont out of his own home. Nor could she give any adequate reason why Jenny should not be allowed simply to speak to him if that was what she wanted.

"Very well," she said at last. "I hope you will not detain the gentleman long, my dear. He always rides at ten, and I am certain that he does not care to have anyone stand in the way of his enjoyment. I will be down directly."

"I feel as though I should apologize for her rudeness to you," Jenny said when her aunt was gone.

He shrugged. "What does it matter?" he replied. "No doubt she thinks she has good reason to dislike me."

Jenny looked at him closely. "You really don't care what anyone thinks of you, do you?" she demanded.

"I care what people I admire think."

"Oh, and are there many of those? People you admire?"

"Fewer than I would like," he told her, coming back into the room and closing the door behind him. A silence rose between them, but it was as though they were speaking to one another on another level. Jenny wished he would not look at her so directly. And she wished he had not shut the door. More than that, she wished she had not asked to speak with him. Actually they had nothing to say to one another. She had only thought up the topic of Dr. Dangle because she wanted to show him that she was not allowing her aunt to wrap her in cotton wool.

"Have you noticed, Miss Allen," he said now, "the tendency our conversations have to become verbal battlegrounds?"

He was right, of course, but Jenny did not care to admit it. She sat down on a chair, very prim and very proper in her pale morning sacque with white lace at her wrists and neck — very prim and proper because the door was closed and she did not want him to think that she was throwing herself at him as Letty had told her so many girls had done.

"I wanted to ask you about Dr. Dangle," she said, being as crisp and businesslike as she could manage. "You gathered from the conversation a moment ago that he attended my uncle last night after an accident. Or to put it more correctly, after my uncle had been set on by footpads and cracked on the head."

"I have been out already this morning," Lord Lamont said, "and I heard the story mentioned. How is your uncle now?"

Jenny assured him that Sir Simon was much improved and would have hurried on to ask the question which was paramount in her mind if he had not interrupted her.

"I gather from what your aunt said here this morning, that Dangle actually intended to operate and that you stopped him. My congratulations, Miss Allen. Even the doctor himself agrees with that. Did you notice that he could not even remember having been at your house?"

Jenny discovered that she had no wish to discuss the part she had played in the events of the evening past.

"I only wanted to ask you, Sir," she said, "how it is that you allow your mother to be attended by him. I do not think I am mistaken in saying that I have seen several signs that you think even less of him than you do of Bath in general."

Lord Lamont did not answer her at once, but his eyes still traced the lines of her face. Increasingly, Jenny was aware that they were alone in this room and that the door was closed. Absurd of her, no doubt, but there it was. She might wish not to be a naive country girl, but that was what she was. What was he thinking? That her question was simply a fabrication to engage his attention? Jenny's temper, never far below the surface, began to rise.

"No doubt it is too private a question for you to answer, Sir," she said more tartly than she had meant to sound.

"It would be easier to answer if I knew why you had asked it," he replied in a low voice. "Are you simply gathering proof to support your aunt's all-too-clear opinion of me, or have you another reason."

Jenny rose and crossed the room, putting as much distance between them as she was able. He would see that there was no ulterior reason behind her having questioned him.

"The other reason is that I would like to be informed if there is some reason that I do not know about for engaging Dr. Dangle as a physician," she said crisply. "Clearly he is incompetent and dirty."

"The same might be said for half the physicians in the city."

"You are a cynic, Sir."

"I have good reason to be one. Dr. Dangle is one of many."

"Surely the others cannot be so often in their cups," Jenny protested. "The man is not simply incompetent. He is a danger. And yet you permit your mother..."

"And you permit your aunt."

"Why, I have no control over her at all."

He smiled that familiar dark, sardonic smile. "My answer is an echo of your own," he said. "She prefers him because he has no scruples whatsoever and can be depended on to support her in any claims to illness she may make. After all, she can see him for what he is. She is no fool."

"Like my aunt!" Jenny demanded. "Is that what you meant to imply."

"I was not thinking of your aunt at the moment," Lord Lamont replied. "But if she actually was about to permit Dangle to operate on her own brother..."

"She was hysterical!" Jenny told him. "No doubt she thought her brother was dying. She was in no fit condition to make a judgement."

He smiled again, went to the door and opened it. "So you defend her," he murmured. "You are a curiosity to me, Miss Allen. Most people can be set in a slot. But you consistently surprise me."

"That is only because I have not decided which slot I intend to fit in," Jenny said, tossing her dark curls.

When she looked back at the door, Lord Lamont was gone. She knew she ought to feel relieved and blamed herself because she didn't. She sat and stood and paced and played a light tune on the pianoforte and, when her aunt finally came down the stairs and said that they were to join Lady Madrigal at the Abbey at noon, Jenny said that she would like nothing better and thought, at the time, she really meant it.

chapter eight

"You have an admirer, my dear Tabby," Sir Simon declared the next morning over breakfast. It was a sunny day, and the fragrance from the roses in the tiny garden outside nearly overpowered the smell of kippers, which Sir Simon preferred above all else for his first meal of the day.

Sir Simon was in fine fettle. The footpads who had taken his purse in the process of their attack had been discovered and brought before the justice the day before with the consequence that he had had returned to him all that he had lost by way of material possession and was awarded, as well, with the promise that his assailants would be punished with all the due process of the law.

"Pray, do not lark with me, Brother," Lady

Blunder replied, allowing Chow-chow to lick butter from her fingertips. "It is not in good taste, I assure you. Besides which, I am still troubled by what Devina told me yesterday."

Jenny flushed and turned her face toward the sunlit window, remembering all too well what her aunt had told her after they had completed their morning activities the day before.

"It has been decided that Oliver will settle himself at last," her aunt had told her while they had waited for sedan chairs outside the Abbey. "Dear Devina has the very person in mind. She is the Honorable Mary Williams. Her father is a baron and most agreeable that the match be brought off. Devina says that she is quite prepared to die in the cause and will, no doubt, do so if her son refuses to make the match. Always before he has made some excuse. But Miss Williams has a reputation as a wit, and she is very beautiful, as well. She arrives in Bath tomorrow with her father's blessing to stay with dear Devina. It will be such a relief for my friend to know that Oliver is finally safely launched."

All of which Jenny had listened to with a heart gone suddenly quite cold. She had seen the way Lord Lamont's mother managed to impose on him as a consequence of her illness, real or imagined, and no doubt were she to make it a matter of her life or death she could succeed in wooing him into marriage, particularly if the lady were a wit and wealthy, as well.

"It is no lark, I assure you," Sir Simon said to his sister with a smile. "You *are* admired. The gentleman has been in Bath these three weeks or more and has kept you under close observation, I understand. He knows your schedule exactly and is always at the Pump Room or an assembly hall when he knows that you will be there."

Jenny had never seen her aunt flush before but she did so now, as prettily as a girl, and pretended to pay all her attention to the lap dog which was attempting to earn more butter by lying on its back and panting heavily, which was the only trick it could perform.

"I thought that we had settled that between us a long time ago, Brother," Lady Blunder said. "You are the handsome member of this family, not me. Let Lady Carew and the others pursue you. I have made my own friends, established a schedule, kept myself busy and entertained. And now you choose to mock me into remembering that I have never had a gentleman offer for me."

It was said so harshly and distinctly that Jenny was shocked into taking a fresh look at her aunt, whose cheeks were still stained with red. It all came back to role playing, she realized. Her aunt saw herself in one way and her brother had proposed her as another, which was enough to shock her, for the moment, into dealing with reality in an unaccustomed way.

"Come," Sir Simon said, rising and making

a rare gesture of intimacy by putting his hand on his sister's shoulder. As for Lady Blunder, she groped under the fichu, which was made of lace, and drew out a handkerchief, which she proceeded to dab her eyes with.

"Come," Sir Simon said again. "I have not the slightest intention of mocking you, my dear Tabitha. But when Lady Carew brought this gentleman to my attention..."

Lady Blunder threw down her handkerchief and pushed back her chair, much to the distress of Chow-chow on whose tail she trod in the process of rising.

"So Lady Carew is behind this!" Lady Blunder cried, pushing her brother aside in order to go to the French door which opened into the garden. "Mind me, Simon, when I say that anything she has told you to tell me about an admirer is a lie! No doubt she wishes it were true. No doubt she wishes that I would marry and leave this house so that she could more easily become the mistress of it. But she will look a long way before she finds a gentleman who will make an offer for me. And she will look a longer way still before she will find one whose offer I will accept. Tell her that, Brother. Tell her I was not amused, as well!"

Jenny would have made her withdrawal at that point, for she thought the moment too personal for her to intrude. This was a side of her aunt which she had never seen, and it dismayed her that she could have thought the older woman insensitive when, clearly, there was so much sensitivity underneath the mask she had assumed. But when she rose from her chair at the table, her uncle made a sign which clearly conveyed his wish that she remain.

"I will not pursue the subject, Tabby," Sir Simon said in his most gentle fashion. "Believe me, I did not mean to upset you. The gentleman I spoke of is real enough and a stranger to Lady Carew until yesterday when he made his indirect application."

"Application!" Lady Blunder cried, staring at him myopically. "I do not understand you. Why should he apply to her for anything?"

"He had discovered that you were my sister," Sir Simon said patiently, "and he had seen me in Lady Carew's company. Yesterday he arranged to be introduced to her at the Pump Room by a friend they have in common for the express purpose of somehow arranging an introduction to you."

Lady Blunder stared at him defiantly. "And you took her word for this, I suppose?" she demanded.

For the first time Jenny realized how difficult it must have been for her aunt when she was a girl. Had she been a man her looks would have served her well enough. But her nose alone must have been enough to preclude the possibility of becoming a belle, and she had no special fortune to attract young gentlemen. As a consequence, no doubt, she had put her faith in people who could not hurt her and preoccupied herself with Lady Madrigal's musical evenings and the like to fill her days and nights. And yet her sensitivity had not been discarded completely. Her brother's comments had clearly stung her to the quick. But surely, Jenny thought, he would not make game of her. They differed sometimes, of course, but she had never heard a truly harsh word exchanged between them.

"I took her word because it is quite true," Sir Simon said. "In fact I met the gentleman myself."

"At Lady Carew's arrangement?"

"Yes. At her arrangement. I am so sorry that that displeases you, my dear. No doubt I was not wise to mention that part of it."

Lady Blunder held herself very stiff and straight. "I wonder if she paid him to do this," she said under her breath. "How clever she is! That would be the ultimate humiliation."

"She has no wish to humiliate you, Tabby," Sir Simon said in such a gentle voice that Jenny felt a wave of affection for him. Surely no one could have been gentler with her aunt than he was being. "If you have no desire to meet the gentleman..."

"Do you think me fool enough to fall in with any of Lady Carew's schemes?" Lady Blunder demanded and, visibly upset, hurried out of the breakfast room. Jenny rose to follow her.

"No, no, child," Sir Simon said, retaking his seat at the head of the table and pouring himself another cup of tea. "I know my sister, and she will be better left alone for a few minutes. I should have guessed that it would upset her. Indeed, Lady Carew's proposal was probably the best. I should have said nothing. We should have simply arranged for them to meet. And then Tabitha could have judged him on his value."

"There really is an admirer then?" Jenny asked.

"But of course there is!" her uncle exclaimed. "Why, you will soon be as bad as your aunt when it comes to suspicion! His name is Mr. Jackson, and he has made his fortune in coal, I believe. He is a simple, direct sort of fellow with not a single fancy trim about him. And, if he is to be believed, he has developed a fiery passion for Tabitha such as all the waters in the Avon could not put out. That is his metaphor, not mine. When he speaks of her, you understand, he waxes close to poetic, or rather as poetic as he can get."

Jenny tried not to look as incredulous as she felt. "Even if you can persuade my aunt that this is not part of a plot by Lady Carew to marry her off," she said, "it does not seem, from your description, that Mr. Jackson, nice as he may be, is the sort of gentleman my aunt would consider."

"Well, I had thought of that," Sir Simon said, fiddling with a spoon. "Tabitha can be a snob at times. That is what you are referring to, I expect."

Jenny took a red rose from the vase on the table and held it to her nose, not knowing how exactly the color of it matched the color of her lips.

"It is too simple to sum up as snobbery, I think," she murmured. "When she spoke to me about being cautious due to such a mix in the society, I think she simply meant that standards had been lowered and that there was more...more danger about than usual. That does not mean that simply because Mr. Jackson deals in coal..."

She broke off, remembering the scorn in her aunt's voice when she had spoken of seeing Letty dancing with the son of an ironmonger.

"How do you think we should set about it then?" Sir Simon demanded. In the bright sunlight the lines on his face seemed deeper than Jenny could remember having seen them before, but he was still a handsome man.

"When you say 'we,'" she asked him, "who do you mean?"

For the first time he seemed flustered. "Well, Lady Carew and myself," he said. "And you, as well, if you will be our ally."

Jenny returned the red rose to the company of its companions and considered. "Perhaps," she said at last, "I take too many liberties, but was there any truth to what my aunt proposed as to your motives?"

"I have no motive but to see her happy," Sir Simon replied. And then he went on quickly. "No, lass, I will be honest with you. There are certain difficulties."

"Having to do with the fact that my aunt and Lady Carew could never share a house?" Jenny asked him, hinting a confession.

"That might indeed be a future consideration," he told her. "But I must ask you to say nothing of it to your aunt. It would throw her into a profound depression, or worse. She has always centered her family life about me. But you must believe that I have no wish to go husband hunting for her. I would not prod her into any alliance she might find disagreeable. But when Mr. Jackson presented himself and declared a passion.... Damme, she is a grown woman and well able to make decisions on her own. But first she must meet the gentleman. And I see now that if either Lady Carew or I were to make the introduction possible she would be prejudiced against Mr. Jackson from the start."

Jenny thought there was a deal of sense in what he was saying. And yet she had never thought to be cast in the role of matchmaker, which was clearly what her uncle was suggesting.

"You did not mention his name to her," she said, "which means..."

"That he could be presented to her in the

usual way without her suspecting that he was the gentleman I mentioned."

"Precisely," Jenny said. "And I would gladly do it were it not for the fact that she knows everyone I have met since I have come to Bath. Had she not kept such a close eye on me the matter would be simpler. But, as things are, I believe she would suspect something was wrong in an instant. Where would I say that I had met him? Besides, lies lead to complications. We would be wise to keep the matter as simple as possible."

Sir Simon never wore a wig early in the morning and now he rubbed his short, grizzled hair with the palm of one hand as though it would help him come up with an idea.

"I could ask one of my friends to introduce Mr. Jackson," Sir Simon said reflectively, "but then she might suspect. My sister is blind about some things and quick when it comes to others. Particularly when she has been put on her guard."

Jenny rose from the table and paced across the floor, a slim figure in her white muslin dressing gown, which was tied at the waist with a blue ribbon.

"And if I were to ask one of her friends, such as Lady Madrigal, to perform the service, they would want to know why," she murmured. "And that would put an end to the game directly."

"Surely you know someone who would not

give the plan away to her," Sir Simon protested. "Someone you could trust."

"There is Letty," Jenny replied. "But of course she will not do in this instance. And then there is..."

"Yes, yes," Sir Simon said impatiently. "Who have you thought of?"

"Lord Lamont," Jenny said in such a low voice that her uncle was forced to ask her to repeat herself. Almost at once she wished she had not spoken his name. But it was true that he would do what she asked him without giving her away. No doubt it would confirm his opinion that everything in Bath was done in an involute way, and perhaps he was right. Certainly there was no longer any reason to feel coy about approaching him since he would so soon be affianced to a certain Miss Mary Williams, who was even now on her way to Bath. But there was no need to even think of that! His future plans did not concern her! Her aunt's happiness was her first regard.

"Lord Lamont, eh?" Sir Simon said. "A good idea that, my dear. She will not connect him with me."

Jenny thought of an objection. "It will not do after all, Uncle," she said. "Her lack of regard for the gentleman might rub off on anyone he introduced to her."

"She only objects to Lamont because he cannot tolerate Bath," Sir Simon assured her, rising to take her hands in his. "And because he speaks quite openly of his objections. If Mr. Jackson is forewarned to sing his praises of the city, Tabby will not tar them with the same brush."

Jenny took a deep breath. "Shall we have them meet at the ball at Wiltshire's tomorrow night?" she asked him.

"The sooner the first step is taken, the sooner the results can be seen," her uncle agreed. "Besides that, you would not believe the fellow's urgency. I believe he may throw himself, all unsuspected, at her feet if he is not introduced immediately."

Hearing Lady Blunder's tread on the stairs, they separated as the conspirators they were, exchanging glances but no other words. And Jenny told herself that if she could only concentrate on this affair it would serve to distract her from any private unhappiness, although what the cause of that unhappiness could be she was sure she did not know.

chapter nine

"*I have just had a request from dear Devina,*"
Lady Blunder said as she joined them, a folded
piece of paper in her hand. The upset of half an
hour ago might never have happened if one were
to judge from her cheerful expression. "It seems
that Miss Williams arrived in Bath last night,
although they had not expected her until today."

"And who is Miss Williams?" Sir Simon demanded, finishing his tea and preparing to quit
the room.

"The young lady Devina is determined that
Oliver will marry," Lady Blunder replied. "Marriage is precisely what that young man needs
to mellow him."

"I have known it to produce quite an opposite
effect on others," her brother muttered. "Oh

well, the best of luck to her, I suppose. Match-making is not part of my scheme of things, but everyone must do as they think best, I suppose."

Jenny nearly gasped at such a display of bold-faced hypocrisy, but her uncle only smiled blandly and left her and her aunt together.

"Dear Devina has asked me if I will see to the gel's entertainment until Lady Lamont can be out and about again," Lady Blunder continued. "She cannot put her in Oliver's care, of course. That would not be seemly. Particularly since they soon will be engaged. In the meantime, the gel cannot be allowed to languish about a sickroom, or so Devina puts it."

Jenny was appalled and could only hope she did not show it. She had no wish to know Miss Mary Williams! Indeed, she had a positive antipathy to the idea. Let her come here and marry Lord Lamont if she liked, but Jenny wanted no part of her. And yet what could she do? Claim illness and have Dr. Dangle set upon her? And even if she were to claim a headache it would only serve for today and be no answer if Lady Lamont decided to keep to her bed for a matter of days.

"I thought we would take her across the river to Spring Garden," her aunt was saying. "It is a sweet retreat on a sunny morning and will make a nice change for you from the Pump Room, my dear."

Jenny was forced to admit to herself that she had some curiosity about the beautiful and witty Miss Williams, but it was not curiosity that made her take a special care with her own toilette or choose to wear the pink and white striped polonaise gown which her aunt had had made for her with its flounces and fur-belows and small hoop which seemed to make her sway when she walked. Much pain was taken to arrange the black curls just so, and she chose to wear the serrated straw hat with the long pink bow.

For this excursion Lady Blunder had the fam-ily's lozenged coach brought to the door, and they took a broader road than Gay Street to the North Parade, where they found Lord Lamont just riding off on a splendid day. The sight of him on horseback was somehow convincing to Jenny that he did indeed belong in the country. She could picture him riding about his estate, glad that here, at least, he could be master. But now that Miss Williams had arrived in Bath the country might not seem so attractive to him. It was a strangely bitter thought.

And then, suddenly, a girl was standing in the doorway, holding up her gown a bit with her gloved hands. A stylish jockey hat adorned a head of golden hair, and her face would have been an example of almost classic beauty had the features not been quite so sharp. Her blue taffeta gown sported an apron made of lace which matched that at her breast and sleeves, and there was a simple strand of pearls around her neck. She was as attractive as Jenny had feared that she would be, and her first words to them proved her wit.

"I thought Lord Lamont might attend us, since we have you as chaperone, Lady Blunder," she said when introductions had been performed and she was seated beside the older woman, opposite Jenny, "but he prefers to ride outside the city at this hour of the morning, and of course, young gentlemen must have their way, particularly if they are rich and handsome."

Lady Blunder, who was clearly prepared to think the very best of the girl if for no other reason than that she was sponsored by her friend, Lady Lamont, laughed at that, but Jenny wondered if it had really been a witticism. Miss Williams must have been told why she was here and what she was to accomplish. But was it wise, Jenny wondered, to be so outspoken, even in appearing to jest? But it was soon apparent that Miss Williams' words were as sharp as her features.

"Now, Lady Blunder," she said, as the coachman turned the carriage in the direction of the bridge, "you must acquaint me with the truth about my hostess's condition. She and my mother are friends, you see, and I know that her health has often been uncertain. But when plans were made for me to come here I did not expect to find her languishing in bed."

All of which was said in such a sarcastic manner, with emphasis on the word "languishing," that Lady Blunder looked quite startled.

"But is she really an invalid?" Miss Williams demanded when Lady Blunder had finished describing her friend's various infirmities. "I will put up with sickrooms if I must, but she has lost my sympathies entirely if she is a hypochondriac."

There was no doubt in Jenny's mind that the young lady meant precisely what she said, but Lady Blunder, accomplished as she was in misreading the character of others, took this outspoken statement as a joke as well. Apparently the possibility that the girl might, in fact, have no use for hypochondria was so foreign to her that she must convert whatever she said into dry wit. As for Miss Williams, she looked a bit startled at being laughed at again and then turned her attention to that part of the city they were driving through.

"How narrow the streets are," she observed. "And the buildings are so very dirty. I had expected to find much more elegance about. Of course, I have spent a good deal of my life in London, and my expectations are high as a consequence. Have you spent much time in London, Miss Allen?"

Jenny confessed that she had not, indeed that she had never been there.

"What!" Miss Williams exclaimed. "Not even for your coming out?"

Jenny guessed that she was on the verge of

being condescended to and decided to be as frank as possible, although she could not imagine what business it was of Miss Williams to know her history.

"My father was a vicar in the North," she said, pursing her lips when she paused in a way which should tell Miss Williams that she did not speak in an idle manner. "Our way of life did not include London seasons. Now that my parents are dead, my aunt and uncle have kindly taken me in. My introduction to society in Bath is my coming out."

"How miserable for you," Miss Williams said with a little sniff. "Bath is such a stuffy little town, and I have heard it said that the hoi polloi are everywhere and that one literally cannot avoid rubbing shoulders with them."

That was almost so precisely what her aunt would say that Jenny waited for an expression of agreement from her. But it seemed that only the first part of Miss Williams' general condemnation had struck Lady Blunder.

"Bath stuffy!" she exclaimed. "Oh, my dear Miss Williams, I had heard you were a wit!"

And once again she broke into a fit of laughter, which caused Miss Williams to draw her sharp features into a frown.

"Is your aunt always this full of general merriment?" she murmured to Jenny. And then, without waiting for an answer, she proceeded to make a running commentary on the general lack of style exhibited by the dress of the pedestrians, while Lady Blunder greeted every observation with amusement.

"What a peculiar bridge!" Miss Williams exclaimed when they reached the river. "An architectural monstrosity!"

"Oh, how you do go on, my dear!" Lady Blunder exclaimed, breathless from laughter. "A monstrosity, indeed!"

"My aunt means that it was built by Robert Adam," Jenny said quietly. "You have heard the name, perhaps."

This was a subtle jab on her part since Robert Adam was responsible for the finest architectural design in England and was acknowledged by everyone to be the master of his craft. In the case of the bridge at Bath, he had been commissioned by Sir William Pulteney and had created a lovely and unusual design. The bridge itself was lined on both sides with graceful houses sporting elegant Venetian windows and domed pavilions at each end, set off by free-standing columns.

Miss Williams bridled. "You know very well that everyone has heard of Robert Adam, Miss Allen," she retorted. "I admire his work as much as anyone. But there *must* be exceptions, and this bridge is one of them. La, I feel quite suffocated, blocked in like this. One might as well be on a narrow street anywhere instead of crossing a river which, although it does not offer the finest prospects, should at least be seen, in my opinion."

Even Lady Blunder could not be deceived into thinking that statement a witticism, and her laughter died away. As for Jenny, her growing irritation with the young lady who sat opposite could no longer be contained.

"Have you seen nothing here to like since you arrived then?" she inquired. "If that should continue to be the case—the disappointment piled on disappointment—no doubt you will not wish to prolong your stay."

"In answer to your question," Miss Williams said with an edge to her voice, "I have indeed seen nothing to approve of yet. As for the duration of my stay, it is kind of you to take an interest in it, I'm sure. But whether or not I like this city has very little to do with my purpose for coming here, as I am sure you know, your aunt being such a great friend of Lady Lamont."

The bridge behind them, they approached the gardens by the river, where a profusion of roses and other flowers filled the soft morning air with a sweet fragrance. But try as Jenny might to concentrate on the beauty of the scene, the sky blue of the water covered with boats of every variety, with the hillside town behind, she could only think of the deliberate calculation of Miss Williams' last words. Clearly she had come here to seek a proposal from Lord Lamont.

And what did he think of her, Jenny wondered? No doubt he would be struck by her beauty. But, more important, he would note that she was as unenthusiastic as he was about

Bath and its society. They would have something in common from the start. Furthermore, there was no doubt in Jenny's mind that Miss Williams would hold her own with Lady Lamont. Obviously she saw her for what she was and would deal with her accordingly. All of which might take Her Ladyship by surprise. But, since she had previously decided that this was the wife her son must have, she would probably be more than willing to make allowances.

"What a direct way she has with her," Lady Blunder whispered to her niece as they descended from the carriage. "That combined with her wit is certain to make her irresistible to Oliver."

Finding that she could provide no argument, Jenny began to agree when Miss Williams, rather more loudly than was required, declared that the gardens were little more than a reclaimed swamp.

"It is certain to be unhealthy here," she said, "even when the sun is shining. It is too low-lying a place to be anything other than extraordinarily dangerous. I wonder that you can bring yourself to come here, Lady Blunder, indeed I do!"

Since they were standing in what was clearly one of the beauty spots in England with dry gravel paths and flowers all around, not to mention trees which were anything but the swamp variety, the notion that they had put themselves in danger was still another dry witticism to

Jenny's aunt, who went off into another gale of laughter.

Having shaken her head in a bewildered manner at Lady Blunder's response, Miss Williams turned to take a condescending look around her and gave an exclamation.

"Good heavens, it is that dreadful doctor who attends Lady Lamont!" she said to Jenny. "I cannot believe that she allows him to attend her. He was at the house very early this morning and, even at that hour, in his cups. And now he is drunker than ever, if appearance is any proof."

Jenny turned and found that it was true. The ubiquitous physician was even now descending on Lady Blunder, who was evidencing every sign of being glad to see him.

"La!" Miss Williams declared, snapping open her fan. "It seems your aunt is enamored with him as well, Miss Allen! I wonder that you have put up with it."

"Yes, I expect you do," Jenny replied coolly and, feeling that she had listened to Miss Williams' general criticism quite long enough for one morning, strolled off alone on the path which led directly to the river, leaving the witty and beautiful Miss Williams to herself.

chapter ten

Although she did not have to engage in conver-
sation with her, Jenny found it was not possible
to put Miss Mary Williams out of her mind.
That evening at the Assembly Rooms, Letty
and her mother were waiting for Jenny in
the entry. For once Lady Carew did not attach
herself immediately to Sir Simon. Instead,
she assisted her daughter in finding the
three of them a quiet place so that they could
talk.

"I heard that you and your aunt were at the
gardens with her this morning," Lady Carew
declared. "My dear, is she as officious and disapproving as she appears?"

There was no need to ask them who they were
talking about, and Jenny did not trouble to
make the pretense that she did not know.

"I take it that you have had occasion to observe Miss Williams," she replied.

Lady Carew was looking even younger than usual, despite her silver hair, which she had piled high on her head this evening and decorated with pearls. "She arrived with Lord Lamont and his mother quite an hour ago," she told the girl. "Everyone is talking about her extraordinary manner."

"I expect she has been dazzling the company with her brilliance," Jenny said more dryly than she had intended.

"Well, as for brilliance, I am not so sure of that," Letty declared in her pert manner. "Certainly she might pass for beautiful. At least that is my decision."

"Her nose is like the edge of a knife," Lady Carew declared firmly. "Besides, I have seen her type before. Every year their features grow sharper until they take on a shrewish look."

And she preened herself contentedly, clearly well aware that a tiny bit of plumpness was in her favor.

"It is her talk which has raised comment," Letty declared. "I take it that she is forthright to the point of rudeness. And that she decidedly does not care for Bath."

"That was my impression," Jenny replied, indicating with a little turn that they should go on into the ballroom. Certainly she had not liked Miss Williams, but she found there was no sat-

110

isfaction for her in standing about and making criticism of the girl.

"In particular she has no patience with Lady Lamont," Lady Carew declared, clearly in no mood to bring a halt to the discussion. "Why, I heard her myself as they came through the door and..."

"I thought that when you mentioned Lady Lamont before, you had made a natural error," Jenny declared. "Surely she is not in attendance. Why, only the other evening at Lady Madrigal's soirée she collapsed completely as a result of making that small effort."

"Oh, she is here," Letty replied. "No doubt about it. That is why they came early, I think, for Her Ladyship is in a Bath chair. She is making the effort for Oliver's sake, she says."

"But why would Lord Lamont care whether or not she came here to a ball?" Jenny demanded, stung out of her reluctance to gossip by the memory of the way Lady Lamont had gone on and on about coming out into society for her son's sake that evening at Lady Madrigal's. "The fact that Miss Williams is a guest and that she cannot come to an affair like this alone with Lord Lamont should not matter, for my aunt offered to be Miss Williams' chaperone on all such occasions."

"She likes to play the martyr," Lady Carew told her. "There is nothing she likes better than to bring her son down from the country by pretending to be severely ill and then to make a show of forcing herself up and out to some entertainment or other 'for his sake.' She is a truly dreadful person and I wonder that he lets her do it. I mean to say, Lord Lamont has a deal of character. A certain strength. I do not know quite how to put it...."

"If you were twenty years younger, Mama, I fancy you would find the precise words," Letty said, softening the impertinence with a loving smile.

Lady Carew made a pretense of striking her daughter with her fan. "What a jade you are, Letty!" she exclaimed. "You have quite put me off my concentration. Oh, yes! I meant to say that I heard Miss Williams myself tell Lady Lamont that she would call the footman and have her taken home to her bed if she heard any more complaints. 'If you are feeling that poorly, Madam,' she said, 'you should be in bed and not in this crowd and heat, which is enough to make anyone feel ill.'"

"You should have seen Lady Lamont's face," Letty declared. "I think that she wanted to be angry, but of course she cannot afford to be. I mean to say, the news is all over town that she has chosen Miss Williams to tempt her son with. It would not do for her to quarrel with her. At least not until after the wedding. Then there will be a blow-up! You can depend upon it. Miss Williams may feel quite free now to fling home truths about with abandon, but it will not be allowed indefinitely."

"I wish I knew how Lord Lamont feels about her," Lady Carew mused. "I have never seen anyone as capable as he of keeping his face quite expressionless. And he is doing that this evening."

Jenny had tried to keep from thinking of Lord Lamont for a good many reasons, the most pressing being her promise to her uncle that she would make use of the young marquess's good offices to introduce Mr. Jackson to her aunt. Now it occurred to her that if Miss Williams was not finding assembly room balls to her fancy, which was apparently the case, and if Lady Lamont thought that she was ailing, the party might take their leave at any moment with Mr. Jackson still not introduced. With this in mind, she took a hasty leave of Letty and her mother, who stared after her in a puzzled way, and followed her uncle's trail into the second entry.

"Ah, here you are, child!" he cried, catching her by the elbow. "I have been waiting for you. This is Mr. Jackson."

The gentleman in question beamed at Jenny and held out his hand for her to shake it. If only his clothing were considered, he could, she thought, quite easily be mistaken for a member of the *haut ton*, but there all resemblance stopped. He was a big, burly sort of man, although that was not the point, and his wiry black hair was so thick and stiff that it appeared ready to burst out of the constraint of powder, sausage curls and queue at any minute. His face was ruddy, either from the weather or a love for ale, and altogether he had a lusty, robust way about him not often found among the older members of the *haut ton,* at least.

But it was his tongue which gave him most away, for it had a common accent to it which was so strong that Jenny did not think he could mask it, even if he had a mind to do so. He was still shaking her hand up and down like a pump handle, all the time showering compliments on her dress and general appearance, all of which, he said, put him in mind of her lovely aunt.

For the first time Jenny realized that the eyes of love see many things in such a way as to bear no real relationship to reality. Among the torrent of words which Mr. Jackson poured out in her aunt's praise, there was not one in fifty she would have chosen to make such a description. According to Mr. Jackson, Lady Blunder was a fairy of delight, an angel to light up his life, a paragon of virtue and the most beautiful woman he had ever seen.

Jenny and her uncle exchanged incredulous glances, but there was no doubting Mr. Jackson's sincerity. Thankfully, he was so intent on his raptures that he did not question why Sir Simon did not simply take him directly to his sister. Indeed, he kept on talking as Jenny led him into the ballroom and looked about for Lord Lamont and his party.

Despite what Lady Carew had said, Miss

Mary Williams was looking quite lovely to-night. Jenny saw her before she could prepare herself for the wave of—not jealousy, she was quite certain of that—severe discomfort which swept over her. Green was Miss Williams' color, and she had made such excellent use of it that she looked like a sea nymph, with stars spun in her fair hair.

"If you will excuse me for a moment," Jenny said, having determined that Lord Lamont and his mother were standing in the shadow of the visiting beauty, who was talking quickly and with a great display of expression to Sir Roger Ramsdale. It was, Jenny thought, as though Miss Williams was determined to keep every eye in the room on her, which was strange, indeed, if she despised the society of Bath as much as she had given indication that she did that morning.

"But Lady Blunder is over there," Mr. Jackson said, pointing straight out with his finger to the other side of the room.

"Yes, yes," Jenny assured him. "I only want you to meet someone else first, Sir."

She groped about in her mind for a reason but could not find one. Instead, she smiled as charmingly as she was able and hurried off to Lord Lamont. She was a slim figure in white, with her dark curls charmingly arranged about her oval face, someone who looked a good deal more confident than she felt.

Jenny had hoped to attract no attention, but

at her approach Miss Williams stopped talking and gesticulating, and Lady Lamont leaned forward in her Bath chair and stared at Jenny curiously.

"I have a favor to ask you, Sir," Jenny said in a low voice, as Lord Lamont moved toward her. "This is...this is awkward for me, but I am doing my uncle a favor."

"In speaking to me, Miss Allen?" Lord Lamont asked. Behind him, Miss Williams and his mother remained watchful, but Jenny was certain that with all the noise there was in the ballroom, including the sound of fiddles being tuned, there was no danger they would overhear her.

"No, no, of course not," Jenny replied, thinking that she could not bear it if he were to be sardonic. "The fact is that someone—a Mr. Jackson—wants badly to be introduced to my aunt. Indeed, he has solicited such an introduction from my uncle. That is the gentleman over there. His name is Mr. Jackson and he deals in coal."

"Why, he is an ambitious man indeed if, dealing in coal, he hopes to cultivate an acquaintance with your aunt," Lord Lamont replied, and she could see he was amused. Indeed, it *was* rather an absurd situation, but it would not do to laugh.

"My uncle only promised to see to the introduction," Jenny replied. "He made no guarantees about what would happen afterward. But

Mr. Jackson is very keen, and, since my uncle cannot perform the introduction and it would be awkward for me, considering that my aunt knows he is not one of my acquaintances...That is to say, my uncle would be very grateful if you would present Mr. Jackson to my aunt. There is nothing more than that to do. It would take only a few minutes and it would..."

She broke off, hating herself for the confusion she was in. She had planned to do this so coolly. She had meant to grit her teeth and go about it as the chore it was. Now, because she had tried to explain too much she had made herself look absurd. What would he think? What *was* he thinking? She could not be certain ever what lay behind those dark eyes. Letty had told her that most of the young ladies in Bath had pursued him at one time or another. Did he think, perhaps, that this was all a last-ditch ploy, a way of hoping to divert his attention from Miss Mary Williams with her beauty and her wit?

But the harm was done now. There was no help for it. Embarrassment led, as usual, to anger, and she began to feel, somehow, that Lord Lamont was at fault.

"Well, Sir," she said, "will you do my uncle this service?"

That was the way she should have done it all. Brisk and businesslike. Not trouble to explain. She forced herself to look up and saw that he was looking past her. "Is that the gentleman?" he asked. "Is that Mr. Jackson?"

"Yes," Jenny said. "He is not being very patient, I'm afraid."

"He looks as though he is having all that he can do to keep from introducing himself," Lord Lamont observed. "Is he a fortune hunter?"

"You may not be able to think of any other reason for anyone to want to meet my aunt, Sir," Jenny said stiffly, "but the fact is that Mr. Jackson has formed a passion for her. Besides, she has no fortune. No more than I."

She had not meant to add that. She bit her tongue when it was too late.

"I had heard just the opposite," Lord Lamont said after a moment's hesitation. "About you, Miss Allen. Not your aunt."

Looking past him, Jenny saw Lady Lamont say something to Miss Williams under cover of her fan, saw that young lady moving toward them. In a moment they would be interrupted.

"Mr. Jackson!" she cried with a lavish fling of her hands. "May I present Lord Lamont. A...a friend. He wishes to have the honor of presenting you to my aunt, Lady Blunder. Come! We must hurry or the next cotillion will be forming and it will be difficult to get across the floor."

Lord Lamont *was* amused! Jenny was certain of it! Oh, how she wished that she could explain that none of this was of her planning. She could imagine the way Miss Williams would greet him on his return from making the introduction. "What a curious little thing Miss Allen is,"

118

she would say, looking as witty and beautiful as possible to mark the contrast. "Whatever did she want you to do?"

And then he would tell her, and they would enjoy a laugh together and add that curious little Miss Allen to all the other things in Bath of which they disapproved.

These thoughts occupied Jenny on their advance across the dance floor and made her so furious that, once Lord Lamont had done what she had asked him to do, presenting Mr. Jackson with no preamble or other explanation in the most self-contained sort of way, she could only thank him stiffly and say she must not keep him any longer. The sardonic look came back into his eyes then, and it hurt her so much to see it that, when he took his leave, she turned away.

chapter eleven

Mr. Jackson's first words, following the introduction, were characteristically frank and to
the point. "I deal in coal, Madam," he said, "and
I have made a fortune out of it."

"Indeed, Sir!" was all that Lady Blunder
could manage. Her nose appeared more like a
beak than ever as she stared at him with myopic
intensity.

"I have no intention of pretending that I do
not have a trade," he told her with an almost
ferocious intensity, which appeared somehow to
extend to the black hair, which seemed about
to throw off his wig. "I am a self-made man,
Madam, and proud of it."

"Are you indeed," Lady Blunder declared,
staring about herself in a wild sort of way, as
though hoping that someone would explain to

her how it was that Lord Lamont should have appeared out of nowhere with this gentleman who dealt in coal, only to introduce him to her and promptly take his leave.

"Not that it will make any difference to you what I do, Madam," Mr. Jackson continued in what was apparently a speech he had memorized for this occasion and now intended to recite in its entirety by rote. "The first time I set eyes on you—it was at the Pump Room on Thursday morning last. I have made a record of the day, you see, and intend to celebrate it annually. As I say, the first time I set eyes on you I knew you were a gentlewoman, someone with finer blood in your veins than me...."

"I do not care to discuss the quality of my blood with a total stranger, Sir," Lady Blunder said in a voice which was not as stern as that which Jenny, standing by her side, had expected to hear.

"Quite so," Mr. Jackson replied, taking the rebuke in bright good spirits. "I must remember that you are delicate and speak accordingly."

Anyone less delicate in appearance than her aunt Jenny had never seen, but she reminded herself that love saw with special eyes and often was called blind.

"As I was saying," the coal merchant proceeded enthusiastically, "the first time that I set eyes on you, I knew that you were of the quality, but there was something about you that told me you were not the sort to give yourself airs and think that just because you have a title before your name you were meant to condescend."

"Well, as for that, Sir," Lady Blunder replied, looking at him as though he were a specimen of some sort which she had never seen before, "I have always been particular about whom I make acquaintance with. Yes. Very particular, I assure you!"

But Mr. Jackson was clearly not the sort to be put off so easily. "I was certain of it, Madam!" Mr. Jackson said, striking the fist of one hand into the palm of the other. "I told myself that you were the sort of woman—excuse the expression but I confess that I do not know what else to call you—who would have a scale of values and judge people accordingly. 'Yes, indeed,' I told myself, 'there is a woman who values people for what they are! There is a woman who knows the proper value to put on loyalty and honesty. There is a woman who stands above the crowd!'"

This last statement was so true in the literal sense that Jenny was afraid her aunt would take some offense, but she only eyed the coal merchant with more curiosity. Clearly he would not allow himself to be labeled and put away as easily as Lady Blunder would like, and, in the meantime, she did not know precisely how to deal with him.

"In a word, Madam," Mr. Jackson continued briskly, as though a business arrangement of some sort was being made, "I was taken with you from the start. I was attracted, Madam! Strongly attracted! Drawn to you! Put it any way you like, I cannot consider living the rest of my life without you!"

He spoke so forcefully that, despite the fiddlers' turning and the general uproar, Mr. Jackson had attracted the attention of quite a number of people standing by, including that of Sir Timity, who had been talking to Lady Blunder when Lord Lamont had made his introduction. Indeed, Jenny realized as she looked about herself, they had become the center of quite a little crowd, at the outskirts of which she could see her uncle and Lady Carew.

"*You* are the gentleman my brother spoke to me about!" Lady Blunder declared with sudden realization in her eyes. "*You* are the gentleman who wants me, Sir, and I will not have it! I suppose Lord Lamont put you up to do it. I always knew there was a cruel streak in him. Yes, he wants to make a fool of me and thinks himself very clever, no doubt, for having found someone like you to do it."

"But, Madam!" Mr. Jackson exclaimed. "You are quite mistaken, I assure you. I was introduced to Lord Lamont by your niece not ten minutes ago, why I do not know. My original application was to your brother, Sir Simon, but he did not seem prepared to make the introduction himself."

"A ruse! A ruse!" Lady Blunder exclaimed.

"And my own brother behind it! But I know who is responsible! Lady Carew has had a fancy to see me humiliated and has talked my brother into doing it. And you, Sir! Whoever you may be! Did you do this for the sheer enjoyment of it or are you being paid? If so, I hope the fee is high for, before I am done with you, you will have earned it!"

And with that she began to set about poor Mr. Jackson with her fan with so much violence that the gentleman was forced to bury his head in his hands, knocking his wig off in the process. Sir Simon pressed forward to attempt to calm his sister, but the sight of him only seemed to increase her violence and renew her energy, and he was forced, instead, to lead Mr. Jackson away for his own protection.

Only when both objects of her wrath were gone did Lady Blunder allow any attempt to calm her. All her friends had gathered around during the fray, and Jenny found herself joined not only by Sir Simon but by the Honorable Tommy Basset, old Lord Russell and Lady Madrigal.

"There now, dear Tabitha," the latter declared. "People are too cruel. Only think, your own brother, too! It will be the talk of Bath for days, my dear. I declare, if I were you I would not know how to hold up my head again."

Thus she proceeded to console her friend until Lady Blunder was near tears.

"I will take you and Miss Allen home in my

carriage," Sir Timity said, presenting his flesh-less form, well-padded with satin and yards of lawn as usual, for her to lean on. "You know that no one will be more sympathetic than me to your predicament, dear lady."

"Yes, yes," Lady Blunder mourned. "No one is more understanding."

"And you can confide in me," Sir Timity went on, gently steering her in the direction of the door. "You can tell me anything."

Jenny, who was following in their wake, de-termined that she would prevent any soul searching which might take place in that gentleman's presence, guessing as she did that everything that he was told would be over the city by the next day. But, during the ride home, at least, there was no need to worry, for her aunt was content to do nothing but wail and wave her turbaned head about in a state of great distraction. And when they arrived at the Cir-cus and Sir Timity introduced the notion that, if he were to come inside, he could offer a friendly ear, Jenny said flatly that she thought it would do her aunt more good to go to bed directly.

Once she and Lady Blunder were in the house, however, Jenny discovered that bed was the last place her aunt wanted to go.

"I shall be here waiting when my brother chooses to return home, as he sometime must," she said with a grimness which was more dread-ful to observe than her previous hysteria. And with that she planted herself on the scarlet and white striped settee in the sitting room to the left of the hall through which Sir Simon must pass to reach the stairs. "Yes, leave the door open, my dear, for I am determined to tell him my *full* opinion of what he has done before I let him sleep tonight."

And with that she settled into a glum reflection, sighing periodically in the most distressing way that could be imagined, leaving Jenny to struggle with her conscience. After the outburst her aunt had made at Sir Simon's mere suggestion that she had an admirer, Jenny told herself she should have known that she would not believe the existence of such a person simply by virtue of seeing him. Her aunt had never been attractive in the ordinary way. She had learned to think of herself as someone no man would fall in love with and, now that it had happened, she could not bring herself to have belief in it. And yet Jenny had ignored the possibility that in getting Lord Lamont to introduce Mr. Jackson she would be instrumental in instigating a scene.

But now the milk was spilled, she told herself; there was no sense in allocating blame. Certainly Sir Simon had not meant to cause his sister pain. He thought Mr. Jackson honest in his declaration, and Jenny was inclined to agree. Certainly the coal merchant had approached the matter in an admirable manner, making no pretense to a position on the social scale which he could not later claim. His error had been, perhaps, in being too blunt and quick in making his declaration. That had been enough to startle any woman. But nothing he had done had warranted quite *such* an outburst. In her mind's eye, Jenny saw her aunt wielding her fan as though it were a deadly weapon, and the memory made her shiver. What could she say that would help in that regard? Every time her aunt would think of what she had done, she would be overcome by humiliation. Jenny hated to admit it, but much of what Lady Madrigal had said in her misguided attempt to comfort her aunt was true. There would be talk. Even worse, there would be laughter. Deep in such thoughts as these, she was startled to hear Lady Blunder declare that, at least, she had had one satisfaction.

And what was that, Jenny inquired, glad to see the older woman's spirits raised.

"Why," Lady Blunder said more cheerfully, "I showed that fellow I would not be trifled with. And in plain sight, too, so that everyone could see that I will not have my dignity impaired! Everyone will think the better of me for it, I am certain. La, but I was that angry, Jenny! I think I beat him about the head with my fan, but I cannot be certain. And Simon was forced to lead the chap away. Retreat from the scene of battle, so to speak, leaving me quite victorious!"

As usual, Jenny thought, not knowing whether to be amused or not, her aunt had managed to see things from the other side of the looking glass. Just as she had reversed Miss Williams' sarcastic chatter into wit, so, despite what Lady Madrigal had said, she viewed her behavior at the Assembly Rooms this evening as a triumph. No doubt in her fury she had not even heard her old friend's dismal prediction.

Jenny had been half convinced that she should do her best to persuade her aunt that Mr. Jackson had meant every word he had to say. But now she was not so certain that she should. At present her aunt was angry at her brother and Lord Lamont for having made her a dupe. She would berate Sir Simon and that would be the end of it. But if she discovered that Mr. Jackson was, indeed, impassioned by her, she would be forced to consider her performance in quite another light indeed. She could consider herself a Joan of Arc of sorts as long as she was convinced that she had been made a fool of. It would be quite different to know that she had publicly scolded a lover, and that her first.

Lady Blunder was wearing a half-smile as she looked into the middle distance, and Jenny imagined that she was recalling her triumph with a degree of pleasure. Oh, what a tangle it all was! Because of Mr. Jackson, who after all was a stranger to her, she had made Lord Lamont think that she was chasing after him like all the others. Yes, she was certain of it. Something about her amused him, no doubt. Certainly it had been kind of him to have done what she asked without asking too many questions. But he must have thought it an extraordinary request, and then to have witnessed the uproar that had followed...! Even worse, the condescending Miss Williams must have seen it. Jenny could just imagine the remarks she must have made. Brilliant gems of wit. Lord Lamont had a sardonic sense of humor. Certainly he would laugh.

Still, what did that matter to her? Jenny went to the window and looked out onto the gently curving Circus, dimly lit by moonlight, and wished that either her uncle would come home and her aunt could have it out with him, thus making it quickly over, or that he would remain away and her aunt would soon claim weariness. Her outrage would have moderated itself the next day. Indeed, she already seemed more at peace with herself, for a smug smile was pulling at her lips. But just at that moment there was the rumble of carriage wheels on cobblestones, and Jenny knew her uncle had arrived. Lady Blunder heard as well and, rising from the settee, she assumed a hostile demeanor.

"Aunt Tabitha!" Jenny cried. "It would be wrong of you to be angry with him. Mr. Jackson is in earnest. I hesitated to tell you, but you must know the truth before you say anything to Uncle Simon which you will regret later. Mr. Jackson has fallen head over heels in love with you."

"You mean to say that that is what my

brother was led to believe," Lady Blunder replied. "Very well, my dear. No doubt you are quite right. Lady Carew is behind this deceit, and I will repay her for it when I have thought of a way. Indeed, if she has paid the fellow to persist in his pursuit of me, I may pretend to take him seriously until I am able to persuade him to confess the truth. Yes, I will mull the notion over tonight. If I can prove that she has made such a contrivance, I will be able to discredit her with my brother soon enough. But that is between you and me, you understand."

Jenny followed her aunt into the hall and saw tne wary look on her uncle's face, as the footman let him in the door, change to one of bewilderment as Lady Blunder, sailing past him on her way to the stairs, blew a kiss.

"Such a delightful evening," she called over her shoulder. "Mr. Jackson seems a charming man. I intend to have him for tea soon if you will find out his address. You should apply to Lady Carew for it, I think. Good night, dear Simon, and sweet dreams."

chapter twelve

"Just as I predicted, everyone is talking about you, Tabitha my dear," Lady Madrigal said with a smug smile. "I knew you would want a friend like me to be the first to tell you."

In honor of Lady Madrigal's visit, they had repaired to the drawing room even though it was early in the morning. The day matched Jenny's mood, for rain was drizzling down the windows and the air was somehow thick and oppressive.

"I am certain that everyone admires my spirit," Lady Blunder replied, peering at her guest and smiling. "There is no need to marvel about it publicly, however, for it is a well-known fact that I insist on maintaining my dignity, at all costs."

Not for the first time, Jenny reflected that

her aunt's mind traveled certain routes so con-volutedly that it was difficult for her to follow its progress. However, it was apparent that Lady Blunder had made her own interpretation of the events of the evening past, and it was unlikely that anything Lady Madrigal could say would make her see it differently.

"Dignity, my dear Tabitha!" Lady Madrigal cried. "How can you speak to me of dignity when you were beating the poor man with your fan?"

"It was all a mix-up," Lady Blunder told her, "and I find I do not care to discuss it. Tell me about the ball, my dear. I wish I had not had to leave so early."

Jenny's mind drifted off on its own course as Lady Madrigal began her recitation. It was strange that so many people here appeared to need gossip to sustain them just as much as they needed food. Still, she supposed that it was only natural for people to be curious. Perhaps it was the day that made everything seem so dark. As for the way she had embarrassed herself in front of Lord Lamont, she *would* not think of it!

Last night, after her aunt had sailed off up-stairs, her uncle had told Jenny how grateful he was that she had done her best to help him. "No doubt Lord Lamont was curious as to why you wanted him to make the introduction," he said.

"I did not give him the chance to ask," Jenny replied, torn between the desire to talk about it and to put the event completely out of her mind.

"Ah, well, I meant to thank him myself and make some explanation," her uncle had said, "but he had left before I could. Mr. Jackson took a bit of soothing as you can imagine. Poor Tabitha. What a pity it was that she should choose to think he was a knave."

Jenny bit her lip to keep from telling Sir Simon that his sister was certain now that Lady Carew was responsible and that her aunt intended to make some punishment or other.

"I can never anticipate what she will say or do," Sir Simon had continued. "I came home tonight with a certain trepidation, expecting her to be in a temper. And instead she goes off to bed as though nothing had happened. Sweetness and Light. Can you explain the transformation, my dear?"

Jenny was very fond of him, but she could not betray her aunt unless she were to discover later that Lady Blunder intended to make a serious folly.

"Well, then, that must remain a mystery," Sir Simon said when she demurred. "After what happened this morning I might have guessed that she might fly into a temper. But I never imagined that she would throw discretion to the winds with quite so much abandon."

"Was Mr. Jackson very much annoyed?" Jenny had asked him.

"Why, he was more puzzled and confused

than anything," Sir Simon said. "'Pon my soul, I thought he was very decent about it. I took the liberty of making an explanation, of course. I thought I owed him that much."

"You mean you told him that your sister kept a very narrow circle of friends," Jenny suggested.

"I did not want to offer him too much discouragement," Sir Simon replied. "I told the straight truth, damme if I didn't. I said my sister had come to think of herself as an unattractive woman over the years."

"What did he say to that?"

"Why, he said he could not believe his ears, that she was one of the most beautiful women he had ever seen. I confess, my dear, that made me suspicious of him. After all, he is not blind. It came to me that he might think she has a fortune, so I disillusioned him on that fine point straight away. I mean to say, I told him that, since she thought she had no looks and knew she had little money, she had long since given up exciting the passions of any gentleman. And, as a consequence, when he made such unexpected protestations, she was more alarmed than anything and strongly suspected a joke."

"And did he believe you?"

"He all but wept," Sir Simon replied. "He told me that was one of the saddest stories he had ever heard and that it only drew him closer to her. Why, he called her 'my dear heart' and dabbed at his eyes until he made me feel quite sentimental about my own sister."

Jenny had thought it was a pity that her aunt had privately decided to take advantage of the gentleman for the purpose of trying to make him admit that Lady Carew was behind his professed passion. But, of course, that was not the way Lady Blunder saw it, and there was no use trying to persuade her otherwise. She could only hope that if Mr. Jackson were as good and decent a man as he appeared, her aunt would come to recognize the fact.

Jenny suddenly became aware that Lady Madrigal had changed the subject of her gossip to Lord Lamont. "They say that he is bound to offer for the girl. And, indeed, she seems quite charming, although perhaps a bit withdrawn. But then, of course, that can be explained by shyness. Even though she does come from London, she must find us a rather sophisticated sort of group."

Jenny would have liked to tell Lady Madrigal how wrong she was but did not think it worth the trouble. Let Miss Williams take Bath by storm, if she pleased. As for herself, she did not want to hear about her. As Lady Blunder began to sing the newcomer's praises, Jenny rose and started toward the door.

"What, are you leaving us, child?" her aunt broke off to ask her. "Are you feeling well?"

"Only a little restless," Jenny assured her.

"I think a stroll would do me good. Just around the Circus and perhaps across to the Royal Crescent. Do you mind?"

Clearly Lady Blunder did not want to be distracted from a gossip with her distinguished friend, and she saw Jenny off with a cheerful wave of her hand, apparently forgetting the rain, which, under other circumstances, would have been certain to make her fuss. In fact, Jenny had forgotten about it herself and was relieved to see, as she went to fetch her cape, that the drizzle had turned into a mist.

It was good to be outside the house, she soon discovered. Good to fold herself into the misty morning and feel truly alone. Ever since she had come to Bath, she realized, she had been in the company of someone, usually her aunt. And, much as she cared for Lady Blunder, Jenny realized that the older woman tended either to confuse or suffocate her. Now that she had had a proper introduction to the city, it would be good for everyone concerned if she took more time for herself, or to be with friends like Letty. No doubt her aunt would put up objections because of her dislike for Letty's mother, but Jenny was determined to make it clear that she must make her own decisions. There would never be another ball, for instance, at which she would agree to take refreshment with someone like Lord Russell who, nice as he might be, was not her choice for the ideal partner.

And if her aunt were truthful with herself,

Jenny thought, turning her face up to the freshness of the mist, she would admit that Jenny did not have to be a burden on her. She could go back to having an exchange of *on dit*s with friends like Lady Madrigal and forget her fears that her niece was about to be pursued by fortune hunters and meet with other dread catastrophes. Then, too, there was the possibility that, given the opportunity, Mr. Jackson might distract her more than Lady Blunder expected. Jenny felt her spirits rise.

The Circus rose high above the city on the side of a hill, and something about knowing that an entire city lay below her, and that she was layered in a cloud, produced its own exhilaration. Indeed, the mist was thick enough to make traffic by carriage difficult, and there was only the occasional sound of horses' hooves on the cobblestones to break the silence. Jenny could just make out the entrance of Brock Street, which led to the Royal Crescent, and she was turning onto it when a phaeton drawn by two horses seemed to materialize out of nowhere, driving dangerously close to the curb. Instinctively Jenny cried out, although the wheel of the carriage only brushed her arm. In that same instant the horses were brought to a stop, and someone was jumping down from the high driver's seat.

She did not know it was Lord Lamont until she heard his voice for the mist had grown almost impenetrable. And it was clear from the

137

way in which he addressed her that he could not see her face.

"Are you all right, Miss?" he demanded. "I could not see you. Indeed, I did not know that you were there until you cried out."

Jenny's first instinct was to get away as quickly as she could without his recognizing her. The hood of her cape was deep, and she had turned her face aside the moment that she heard his voice.

"I am quite all right, Sir," she murmured. "Please be on your way."

"I must be certain," he insisted. "It was entirely my fault and I accept all responsibility. I was just returning from an early call at the house of a friend who lives on the Crescent. If you will go there with me, we can see..."

So much solicitude for a stranger was a virtue, Jenny told herself, but awkward in the circumstances. For all he knew she might well be a servant girl. And he was making it very difficult for her to preserve her anonymity.

"No, no!" she exclaimed. "Even if my arm were bruised, I live there in the Circus and could easily have it attended to."

Later she was to wonder whether she had deliberately given herself away. "Miss Allen!" he exclaimed. "How extraordinary. I recognize your voice now. It's Oliver Lamont."

As though even the weather was scheming against her best intentions, the rain chose just that moment to come down in a downpour which would have drenched them both in minutes if Lord Lamont had not quickly drawn Jenny inside the carriage.

"Let us wait for a few minutes and see if it does not let up," he murmured. And, although Jenny wanted to protest, she knew that it would have been an absurd thing to do. It was only sensible to sit here with him for a few minutes and wait. Even her aunt, were she to know about it, could scarcely disapprove.

A silence fell between them, which was ironic, Jenny thought, since there was so much to say. Surely she should take this opportunity to explain to him the reason she had made her strange request the night before. But somehow she was loath to do it. It seemed too much like raking over old coals.

"You and your aunt were good to keep Miss Williams company the other morning," he said finally. There were shadows in the covered carriage, and she could not see his eyes. But his voice was level, as expressionless as his face had been the night before. No doubt, Jenny thought, he could think of nothing more boring than trying to make conversation with a young lady whom he scarcely knew because of a rain shower. And yet she wished that he had thought of something other to discuss than Miss Mary Williams. The rules of polite discourse dictated that she say something about how pleasant it had been, but she discovered that she could not force out the lie. Instead, she came directly to the point.

"My aunt considered her a wit," she said, "but it seemed to me that she was very discontent with this Society. Certainly she was critical enough of it."

There was a pause. "Yes," he said at last. "Miss Williams *is* critical. She is a young woman who knows her mind."

Jenny flushed and was glad he could not see it. He was contrasting her to his house guest and had found her wanting. Their last discussion had made it clear that she had no well-formed opinions. She remembered the way Lord Lamont had looked at her when she had complimented Sir Timity and the Honorable Tommy Basset on their musical performance.

"Since you both think so little of this city," Jenny said without meaning to, "you and Miss Williams must have a great deal to talk about."

It was the first thing that had come into her mind and she had said it. Another gaucherie! And, since the rain was still pounding down, there was no escape.

"I have no quarrel with Bath itself," Lord Lamont replied slowly. "In itself it is a fine enough place. And if I seem to disapprove of the way people conduct themselves, it is only my opinion, and no doubt I should keep that to myself."

She wished that she could tell if that sardonic

look was in his eyes. Or perhaps it was just as well she did not know.

"And what of you, Miss Allen?" he said. "Are you happy here?"

How desperately he was trying to make the conversation "go," Jenny thought. To ask her if she were happy, as though she were a child, without really wanting to hear the answer. Still, she was determined to be honest. What did it matter, after all? The rain could not keep up at this rate for much longer and they would part. Perhaps by the next time she saw him he would be affianced to the witty and beautiful Miss Williams.

"Life is difficult enough," she said, thinking of her aunt and the unhappy romance which had done so much to form her present character. "If people can come here and take part in a play of manners which allows them to forget reality—or perhaps to feel that by being at the Pump Room at nine in the morning and the Assembly Rooms at eight at night they are somehow in control of their own destiny—then I have no quarrel with them."

"And if, in the process, they establish false values and continually deceive themselves, what do you say to that?"

"I cannot judge the values of others exactly," Jenny told him. "It would seem to me enough that I know what I believe in, such things as honesty and kindness and loving one another

141

when we can. No doubt I strike you as curiously naive, Sir."

"On the contrary," he said in a low voice. "You have simply not discovered your own complications and, with any luck, perhaps you never will."

Jenny felt a curious moment of anxiety, as though they had strayed too close to the edge of truth telling. They did not know one another well enough for that. They never would.

"The rain is slackening!" she exclaimed. "I do not mind a little wetness. Indeed, I thought I should suffocate in the house this morning. Thank you for the shelter, Lord Lamont."

And, ignoring his protests that she allow him to drive her home, she stepped down to the curb before he even had a chance to help her. She had nearly reached her aunt's house on the Circus before she heard the wheels of his phaeton begin to roll.

chapter thirteen

The whist party that afternoon which took place in the card room at the new assembly hall called the Upper Rooms was crowded, due in part, no doubt, to the continued inclemency of the weather. Jenny accompanied her aunt through the charmingly decorated octagonal anteroom, past the ballroom on the left and the tea room on the right, straight ahead into the charming card room where four musicians were playing in the gallery and the portrait by Gainsborough of Captain Wade, Master of Ceremonies, looked down on the whist players. Jenny caught a glimpse of Miss Williams across the room, staring disdainfully about her, as though making silent criticism of the four marble fireplaces or the glittering, central chandelier. Jenny looked in another direction immediately, not wanting to know whether or not the girl was in the company of Lord Lamont.

She had not told her aunt about her accidental meeting with him this morning. Somehow she was certain that he would mention it to no one else, and the mist had made it their secret as far as any casual observer was concerned. After all, nothing really happened. His carriage had loomed up out of the silver dimness and startled her. And then he had sheltered her from the rain. Their talk had been nothing but the sort of idle exchange which might have taken place between two strangers anywhere. That was what she told herself, at any rate.

Besides, her aunt had not really given her an opportunity to say anything at all, full as she had been of Lady Madrigal's plans to give a gala for the same Miss Mary Williams Jenny had just glimpsed.

"Dear Devina wants to make her feel as welcome in Bath as possible," Lady Blunder had said as Jenny had given the footman her wet cape. "If she becomes fond enough of the city, we can depend on her and Oliver being here far more than he has ever been in the past. Lady Madrigal thinks that she will be the most excellent wife imaginable for him."

"Being both witty and beautiful," Jenny had said dryly.

"Yes, there is that, of course," Lady Blunder had said quite seriously. "But Lady Madrigal thinks that will cajole him into being fonder of Society than he has been."

Jenny did not expect that Miss Mary Williams had probably ever in her life cajoled anyone. Cajoling was not her way. As for her fondness for Society, that was restricted to the London *haut ton,* judging from what she had had to say. But Jenny had said nothing to dispute her aunt. And, as for the depression which had settled over her, there was nothing to that except the general grayness of the day.

Now, in the brighter confines of the card room, with the gentlemen in silks and satins and the ladies gay as peacocks, with the hum of conversation making a duet to the music, the slap of cards, the laughter, Jenny determined to be happy. And with that end in mind, leaving her aunt to settle at one of the tables with some friends, she went in search of Letty and found her almost immediately.

"I am so glad to see you," Letty cried as they embraced. "What a pretty polonaise. But then blue becomes you since it matches your eyes. Do you like my Leghorn hat? Mama allowed me to come alone. Only imagine! Your aunt would think that quite the worst thing in the world and so you must not tell her. And do not breathe a word about the fact that Mama is going to the concert, for I think your uncle is going there, too."

And so Letty rattled on at a great rate, making a great show of being in the best of feelings, but gradually it bore in on Jenny that something must be very wrong indeed to account for so much nervousness and a general pallor.

"There are Lord Lamont and Miss Williams," Letty declared, nodding to her right. "See, they are sitting down at cards with his mama and Sir Roger Ramsdale. I do not think I have ever seen Lord Lamont in the card room here before. Miss Williams is making a great change in him."

Jenny made no answer for, at that moment, Lord Lamont looked up from his cards and his eyes met hers. There was no expression on his handsome face, but his eyes seemed to be saying something. And then she forced herself to look away, forbidding her imagination to run away with her. Her fancy might play the romantic, but the facts told her quite another story. His mother was well enough again to attend balls and play a public hand again. Always in the past, on her recovery, he had returned to his country estate. This time he lingered on in Bath. Miss Williams must be the attraction that kept him here. There could be no other answer.

"Must we stay on here to talk?" Jenny said suddenly, cutting off Letty's flow of speculation about Lord Lamont and Miss Mary Williams. "It is so crowded."

To which Letty suggested the tea room, which Jenny discovered to be a two-storied colonnade at the west end of the Assembly Rooms with the elegance of an order of Corinthian columns

146

mounted high so that they came immediately below the prettily molded ceiling. Out of sight was to be out of mind, she told herself firmly as she and Letty took a table. She did not intend to as much as utter Lord Lamont's name, and she would not allow her friend to do so, either.

But, as it happened, Letty wanted to speak of quite a different matter.

"If I tell you something in confidence," she said when they had been served their tea, "do you think that you could keep it secret? No matter what happens in the next few days?"

She sounded so much as though she expected tragedy that Jenny's own troubles took wing.

"Yes, I could," Jenny replied. "But you sound as though something quite dreadful was about to happen."

"I suppose from Mama's point of view it will be dreadful," Letty replied and then fell silent. There were very few other people taking tea so early, and the graceful room had a deserted air about it. "She will be betrayed, I know," Letty went on finally. "She has always given me so much freedom. Trusted me. You felt you had to tell your aunt we meant to take tea here before we left the card room, for example. My mother never worries about me. And now..."

"You mean to do something she disapproves of," Jenny murmured.

"I mean to marry a man she disapproves of," Letty said quickly, pushing back the tangle of red curls which fell about her shoulders. "You have not met him for he has been away at London. We thought we had parted for ever, but our letters have served to bring us closer than before. I know you probably think me a feckless person, Jenny, and quite, quite irresponsible, but I do love him so. His name is Captain David Walker and he served in the American campaigns."

"What is there about him to make your mother disapprove?" Jenny asked her. "Indeed, your mother is so liberal in her outlook that it must be something singularly disagreeable."

"On the contrary!" Letty cried, her green eyes flashing. "We are a perfect match. Oh, he is handsome, Jenny, and so brave."

Jenny frowned. "In that case," she told her friend, "he sounds quite eligible enough, unless, that is, your mother is set on your marrying a title."

"Oh, my mother is no snob," Letty replied with a toss of her red curls. "Simply because my father was a viscount does not mean that I must marry into the aristocracy as far as she is concerned."

"Then what objection has she?" Jenny demanded, intrigued.

"It is because David is so brave," Letty said with a little sigh. "He made the mistake of telling her about some of the risks he took in the American campaign. She says she does not wish to see me widowed if there is another war. That is the long and short of it."

"I see," Jenny said thoughtfully. "Well, there is something to that. All the same, if you truly love him and do not mind anxiety..."

"That is what I have tried to tell her," Letty cried. "But she will not listen. It is the only thing I have ever known her to be quite unreasonable about. We quarreled over it, and then she went to David and told him that it was unfair to press me. And she convinced him. That was a month ago. He went away to London, and she told me I must try to forget him. And I *have* tried, but it is useless. I do not want to spend my life with any other man."

Jenny sipped her tea and considered the difficulty. Letty had not asked her for advice, and she did not intend to give it. It was a sad dilemma. She knew how close Letty and her mother were. Remembering her own mother, she realized how dreadful it would have been if she had been put in the same position. But perhaps it was even worse to give up a true love, not knowing whether another would ever come along.

"Oh, it is so good to confide in someone," Letty said, and Jenny saw that her eyes were filled with tears. "The arrangements have been made. On Saturday night I will go to Simpson's with Mama as usual to dance. You know she never keeps her eyes on me. David will be waiting for me outside, and we will leave as soon as I can slip away. That will give us four hours to make a start before she misses me when the ball is over. I will arrange for one of the servants there to give her a note explaining everything."

"But where do you intend to go?" Jenny demanded.

Letty dabbed at her eyes with the lace which hung from her sleeve. "To Gretna Green on the Scots border," she whispered. "We can be married there without a license. Then we will return by way of Yorkshire and break the news to David's parents. He assures me that they will be pleased."

"But your mother..." Jenny began.

"She will be upset, of course," Letty replied, continuing to blot her tears. "But she knows I will be safe with David. It is not as though I were running off with some blackguard or other. And we will return to Bath directly after we have seen David's parents. I can only hope she will be reconciled to it by then."

Jenny realized that, whether she knew it or not, Letty had placed a responsibility on her shoulders. She did not intend to tell her aunt, but she knew what Lady Blunder's advice would be. She would insist that Lady Carew be warned, much as she disliked her. And perhaps that was the right thing to do. But, as it was, she must make her own decision. She had allowed Letty to confide in her. That was as good as a promise to keep her secret.

"You will not give me away," Letty said suddenly, as though they had shared the same thought. "Even if you do not think it wise of me, you will not give me away."

Jenny assured her friend that she would not, but she was troubled all the same. Who would have ever guessed that Letty, with her light-hearted ways, should be considering such a dramatic step! And what a scandal there would be when the word got out! No wonder Letty was in such a state.

And so she helped to calm her and, because they knew it was expected of them, the two girls made their return to the card room, where they found the whist games still in progress. At Lord Lamont's table, Miss Williams wore a self-satisfied smile which told the world that she was winning heavily. The Honorable Tommy Basset suddenly appeared to say that he needed a partner, and, flashing a brilliant smile which only Jenny knew she did not mean, Letty agreed to be it.

Only when she had been left alone did Jenny make her way to her aunt's table, aware that Lord Lamont was watching as she crossed the room. What would he think if he knew Letty's secret, she wondered? Would he think her flighty, manage to throw, somehow, a cynical light on it? It was odd, Jenny thought, how strongly she would like to confide in him. But she was only being silly. What would he care about either her or Letty and their problems?

And then Jenny caught her breath when she saw that her aunt had a new partner. Mr. Jackson sat across the table from her, his broad face flushed with enjoyment. So her aunt intended to follow the course she had set herself the night before. She was determined to lead the poor man on in hopes to prove that his pursuit of her was a game Lady Carew had set him on.

Indeed, the unlikely combination was attracting some attention, which was not unnatural, probably, when so many of the card players must remember the scene of the night before quite vividly. Probably they chalked it up to Lady Blunder's well-known eccentricity that she should partner the very gentleman she had set on.

"My dear!" that gentlewoman cried as Jenny approached the table. "What a long time you have been! I have been fretting so about it that I could scarcely attend to my hand, although Mr. Jackson chides me for excessive anxiety."

Jenny thought that her aunt looked more attractive than she had ever seen her, as though the unaccustomed task of a flirtation had softened her blunt features. Although just now it was difficult for her to think about anything but Letty and her secret, the thought did come to her that, all unintentionally, the older woman might find that she genuinely enjoyed the attentions of Mr. Jackson, who certainly seemed willing to oblige in anything as he picked up her fan when she dropped it and dealt her cards with a special care.

"Just one more hand and we will be going,

child," Lady Blunder said, peering myopically at her fresh cards. "Mr. Jackson will be attending Lady Madrigal's soirée on Friday. I have assured him that I can arrange an invitation for him quite easily. I have told him that no doubt he will see his old friend, Lady Carew there, although he professes not to know who she might be."

Suddenly Jenny remembered all too vividly that moment in the mist-bound phaeton that morning when Lord Lamont had said he had no quarrel with Bath as a city but that he did not care for the conduct of those who lived there. This was the sort of thing he meant then. Another one of all the endless games played in Society. And she had spoken of the virtues. Honesty and kindness and all the rest. What a perfect fool he must have thought her. And, no doubt, with reason.

chapter fourteen

It was clearly with reluctance that the witty and beautiful Miss Mary Williams allowed herself to be the guest of honor at Lady Madrigal's soirée on Friday evening. Just as Jenny had feared, it was to be another musical entertainment, not unlike the first she had attended. The Honorable Tommy Basset and Sir Timity created a sensation with their rendition of a Spanish country dance which demanded an intricate fingering of the lute and a great deal of whirling and twirling about on Mr. Basset's part to exact the maximum effect from his castanets, following which the doleful lady sang another pastoral of her own composing and Lady Madrigal honored them with a medley of love songs which seemed to go on forever.

In the past few days, Jenny had come to wish

that Society in Bath did not move in such restricted circles. Her aunt might complain that everywhere one rubbed shoulders with the hoi polloi, but it seemed to Jenny that wherever she went she saw much the same company. In particular she wished that she would not so often find herself encountering the Lamont party. Of course, in this instance, since Miss Williams was the guest of honor, she was not surprised to see her, but it gave her no particular pleasure.

"How very grim she looks," Letty whispered to Jenny, nodding in Miss Williams' direction. "She could at least pretend to enjoy herself. They say that Lord Lamont enjoys her company, but I certainly cannot understand why."

Lady Madrigal was making such extraordinary sounds as she groped for the upper register that it was quite possible for the girls to talk in low voices behind their fans.

"No doubt she is quite a different person when she is alone with him," Jenny said, privately hoping that it was not true. She had found Miss Williams most disagreeable, and she could not help wishing that Lord Lamont saw her that way, too. But clearly he did not. There was his mother, not even resorting to a Bath chair now, and he was still in the city. Jenny forced herself to remember that that was scarcely her concern.

Following Lady Madrigal's exhaustive performance, there was a surprise. With her breast still heaving from her exertions, their hostess announced that the guest of honor, Miss Mary Williams, had kindly consented to play the pianoforte and sing for them. A spatter of polite applause followed this announcement which Lady Madrigal broke into to add that Miss Williams wished her to announce that she had had the good fortune to study under the famous Mr. Burney, organist at Saint Paul's in London and the most accomplished music teacher in the country, as well as counting among his close friends—and here Lady Madrigal consulted her notes—such famous personages as Johnson, Garrick, Gibbon, Reynolds and Sheridan, the playwright-politician. It was a strange bit of information for Miss Williams to have provided her hostess, Jenny thought, while noting that the general impression had been left on everyone that Miss Williams knew those distinguished people, too.

So, she was a snob as well as being critical and determined. Jenny thought that, given time, she could acquire rather a lengthy list of unfortunate qualities to attach to the character of the witty and beautiful Miss Williams. Still, she *was* undeniably beautiful and, no doubt, could be witty when she chose, and now she was about to prove herself a brilliant musician.

As it turned out, however, that was not quite the case. Certainly Miss Williams gave a flawless performance. The tempo was precisely what it should be. Not a false note was struck. And her voice did the correct things, too. The songs she chose from *The Beggar's Opera* were certainly demanding and, particularly in comparison with the amateur performances that had preceded hers, the word "brilliant" might almost be applied. Almost, but not quite, Jenny thought as she applauded, because there was no feeling there, nothing to thrill you. But it was correctly done. Miss Williams must put a high price on correctness, she thought.

During the encore—for there was one—Jenny forced herself to admit that, all in all, Miss Williams was something of a prize. Her features might be too sharp, as Lady Carew claimed, but seen in silhouette as they were now as she sat at the pianoforte, she was quite stunning. And her figure, in her white satin gown, was certainly appealing. The bored expression which she had worn when listening to the others had been replaced with a carefully measured smile, both when she greeted her audience and later when she made a bow. Jenny happened to glance at Lord Lamont as Miss Williams took her applause, but she could tell nothing from his expression. Certainly, he must have been impressed. Clearly his mother, who sat beside him, was delighted, for she was pounding her hands together with more energy than it might be thought that anyone in her delicate condition might possess.

"Lady Lamont must be thinking that she has backed a winner this time," Letty remarked. She was looking pale, Jenny thought, but perhaps she only imagined it because she knew the strain her friend was under. Still, she had been careful not to speak of it for two good reasons. In a situation like this, anything they said might be overheard. And, because she knew that if Letty wanted to discuss that subject, she would raise it.

"You mean that she has chosen a matrimonial candidate for him before?" Jenny asked her.

"Several times that I know of," Letty replied. "Their arrival is always timed to concur with one of her attacks which bring her son in from the country. But always before..."

"Yes," Jenny murmured, ready to know the worst.

"He has always returned to his estate directly after his mother showed improvement," Letty replied. "Whether there was a guest or not."

That was too exactly what Jenny had suspected to come as a surprise. But now that she knew that he had fled from others, the fact that he was remaining in the city now took on a new significance.

"They say that Miss Williams is responsible for Lady Lamont's return to health," Letty told her friend. "Apparently she has no patience with sick people and, once she made that clear, Her Ladyship had to get on her feet again in order to keep her here."

Remembering, as she did, Miss Williams' reference to a specific reason for having come here, a reason which had very little to do with whether or not she liked Bath, Jenny found herself doubting whether the young lady would have carried out her threat and gone away under any conditions. What a triumph it would be for her to capture a man of the sort everyone but Lady Blunder admired. Handsome. Wealthy. No doubt those were the virtues Miss Williams would admire. Those and his rank. Did she know that he was gentle, Jenny wondered? Did she know how soft his eyes and voice could be?

The applause had ended, but now Miss Williams was surrounded by people like Sir Timity who were extending congratulations. She smiled and nodded at everyone like an animated doll, but there was something in her eyes which told Jenny that she did not much care for the opinion of these people.

"There is something I do not care about in that girl," Lady Carew declared, appearing on Sir Simon's arm. As usual, when he was in her company, Jenny's uncle looked unusually fit and, as for Lady Carew, she might have been a girl had it not been for her silver hairs. Tomorrow night at just about this time those eyes would be glistening with tears instead of happiness. The same thought must have come to Letty's mind for, with no apparent reason, she rose and embraced her mother very tightly about the neck as a child might do.

"La, you must want a favor, Letty," Lady Carew said, laughing and hugging her in turn. "Very well. Out with it. What is it to be?"

Letty looked at her for a moment with a mute appeal in her green eyes, and Jenny knew that she was wondering what would happen if she should tell her mother what she wanted, if she should whisper David's name and try to explain how much she needed him. But then the moment passed. Letty must be certain that her mother would never agree.

Besides, there was to be no time for confessions, for just then Lady Blunder descended on them with Mr. Jackson in her wake.

"Lady Carew!" she cried. "Here is Mr. Jackson, as you see. I know you two are old friends, although he professes not to remember. 'She will be so glad to see you,' I told him. No doubt you will have a deal to talk about, discussions over certain projects you have put afoot."

Lady Carew looked mystified. "But Mr. Jackson and I have never met till now," she said. "Why on earth should you think we had plans to discuss, Lady Blunder?"

Jenny saw Sir Simon nudge Lady Carew and realized that he had seen through what his sister was trying to do. But nudges would do little to solve an awkward situation, as Lady Blunder made clear.

"Never fear, Lady Carew," she said with the hint of a threat in her voice although she continued to smile. "Mr. Jackson will tell me your little secret in good time. Now, come with me and congratulate Miss Williams, Sir, and then we will have a cup of tea and you can tell me all about coal. Mr. Jackson deals in coal, Lady Carew, but then, of course, you know even more about that than I do."

And, with that parting thrust, she hove off through the crowd with Mr. Jackson barging after her, a bewildered expression on his ruddy face.

"My dear," Sir Simon said to his companion, "let me explain."

"By all means do!" Lady Carew declared with energy. "I can make nothing of your sister sometimes. Letty feels the same."

And turning, to draw her daughter in the conversation, she looked for her in vain.

"She must have wandered off somewhere while my aunt was talking," Jenny told her. "Shall I go and find her for you?"

Lady Carew laughed her youthful laugh. "No, my dear. I never interfere with her at entertainments. And, besides, she can be trusted."

It was an irony that she should say that on the night before the night she would be deceived, and Jenny wondered whether Letty could have held to her resolve to make an elopement if she had heard it. Turning away in order to leave her uncle with Lady Carew to explain her aunt's peculiar behavior, Jenny found herself face to face with Miss Mary Williams and Lord Lamont.

It was the first time she had had occasion to be in the company of both of them at once, and Jenny minded it more than she had thought she

161

would. It did not matter that in the mirror which hung above the fireplace she could see herself and Miss Williams reflected in a way that courted comparison. Miss Williams' pale, fair hair was swept fashionably high on her head, and Jenny's curls were held with a band of primrose velvet. Her face was flushed while Miss Williams' complexion was as pale and smooth as her musical rendition had been. Her classic features served as a contrast to Jenny's full lips and retroussé nose. Telling herself that she was a match for this cold beauty in looks, at any rate, Jenny offered Miss Williams congratulations on her performance. Lord Lamont watched her closely, as he always seemed to, and she wondered if he were remembering the other evening when she had praised the Honorable Tommy Basset and Sir Timity and he had thought her hypocritical. Would he wonder how much truth there was in the praise she offered Miss Williams now? Because, in a sense, she lied as much as she had on that other evening. She had not enjoyed Miss Williams' singing. But she could not have explained the reason precisely even to herself.

Miss Williams accepted the congratulations with her customary aplomb and mentioned the fact that, in London, amateur musicals were not at all the fashion.

"I am certain that you find Bath rustic in a good many regards," Jenny retorted. "For me, of course, it is a cosmopolitan existence. But then, I am an impressionable country girl."

She kept her voice quite even and a smile on her lips. There was no sign of sarcasm in her expression, and, after a startled pause, Miss Williams apparently concluded that she could take her at her word. "In that case, Bath does very well for you, I'm sure," she murmured. "If you will excuse me for a moment, Oliver, your mother is calling me. No doubt she wants some reassurance about her health."

She said it in an impatient sort of way. That was the first thing to strike Jenny. The second was that she had called him Oliver. And that could only mean that an engagement would be announced. So it was settled! A great sense of emptiness settled over her. Of course, it meant nothing to her, his engagement. She hoped they would be very happy.

Jenny had expected that Lord Lamont would follow Miss Mary Williams, even though she had not asked him to. But, instead, he remained standing just beside her.

"I did not suppose, somehow, you could be caustic, Miss Allen," he said in a low voice. "I suppose you thought that Miss Williams meant to condescend."

So he did not call her Mary. Not in public yet, at least. No doubt when they were alone together...But she would not think of that. Her mind was in a turmoil. He had noticed her sarcasm, even if Miss Williams had not. And he meant to defend that...that woman to her. Why, it was more than she could bear!

"The little I have seen of your Miss Williams," Jenny flared, "has convinced me that she does very little else but condescend. And, as for being caustic, it *is* new to me. But since I am not witty, it will be a useful enough accomplishment, I warrant."

"And what has being witty to do with anything?" he asked her, frowning.

"Why, you should be the one to tell me that, Sir," Jenny declared, "since you are in such constant contact these days with wit."

How unlike this was to their exchange in a mist-bound carriage only a few mornings ago. And it was, Jenny realized, primarily her fault. Still, she could not endure listening to him justify Miss Williams' attitude. And she had said her bit to that effect.

"If you will excuse me, Sir," she said, "I must..."

But what was there she must do. He stood quite motionless, waiting for her to tell him. Waiting for her to make an even greater fool of herself than she had already done.

"I have a temper," Jenny surprised herself by saying.

"I noticed," he replied.

And with that uncertain pax between them, they took a wordless leave of one another.

chapter fifteen

The morning of the day Letty meant to elope,
Jenny and her aunt followed their usual custom
of beginning the morning at the Pump Room,
an entertainment which Jenny would have still
found beguiling had it not been for her memo-
ries of the night before and the verbal attack
she had made on Miss Williams. Try as she
could, it was difficult to forget what she had
said and Lord Lamont's reaction to it. Thus it
was that she looked about for anything to distract her and chanced to see Dr. Dangle.

It was so clear that something quite dreadful
was wrong with him that Jenny caught Lady
Blunder's arm and pointed in his direction. The
physician had never been noted for the care he
took with his toilette, but he had reached new
heights—or depths—today in the degree of his

disorder. His periwig had been put on every which way, and his face had not been shaved. As for his cravat, no attempt at all had been made to tie it, and it hung down to his waist on either side. The doctor's waistcoat was unbuttoned, disclosing the wrinkled condition of his shirt, and his coat seemed to hang half off his shoulders, as though he had not had the strength to pull his arms completely into the sleeves. One leg of his pantaloons was hiked above his knee, and the other hung so far below that the stocking was scarcely visible. The other stocking had dropped down to his ankle, disclosing a pale and hairless calf. As for his shoes, the buckle had fallen off one and the heel had left the other, making his walk a hobble. No longer was he taking his medicine surreptitiously, but holding the bottle openly. As Jenny and Lady Blunder watched in horror, he raised it defiantly to his lips and drank copiously.

"Dr. Dangle does not appear to be himself, my dear," Lady Blunder murmured anxiously, peering at him myopically.

Jenny thought it would be more accurate to say that he was even more himself than usual, but she kept such thoughts to herself, instead suggesting that they should try to do something to help him.

"Of course! Of course!" Lady Blunder declared, making her ponderous way across the room with Jenny following in her wake. "I never thought to see the dear doctor in this condition. Why, I declare, I think he has been drinking!"

The ladies and gentlemen who filled the hall had not failed to notice the physician's condition, and some were watching him and making comment, laughing or frowning, whichever their wont. Some others preferred to ignore the spectacle he was making of himself, Lady Madrigal and her little coterie among them. But Lady Blunder's faith in the doctor was so completely absolute that she never hesitated, but went to him and took his arm. At close proximity there was no doubt at all that he had been consuming gin in quantity, and Lady Blunder pressed her handkerchief to her nose.

"Let us help you to some place quieter, Dr. Dangle," Jenny proposed, taking him by the other arm, whereupon he gave up the effort to support himself entirely and would have fallen to the floor if Mr. Jackson had not appeared from nowhere and gripped the doctor about the waist.

"Thank goodness!" Lady Blunder cried. "Support him over to that corner, do! There is a chair for him! Give way, please! Give way! This gentleman needs a chair."

This declaration aroused some rowdy comment from a few young gentlemen nearby, but in no time at all, Mr. Jackson had propped the doctor in one of the straight-backed chairs which lined the wall and had relieved him of his bottle, which, at all events, was nearly empty.

"This is my physician, Mr. Jackson," Lady Blunder announced by way of explanation, as Dr. Dangle began to snore.

The coal merchant expressed his amazement that such should be the case.

"His condition is unusual," Lady Blunder continued earnestly. "Usually he is the very soul of propriety."

Mr. Jackson, who already apparently knew Lady Blunder better than she imagined, glanced for confirmation at Jenny, who indicated by her expression and a slight shaking of her head that such was not precisely the case at all.

"We shall have to find out what on earth has happened to him," Lady Blunder told them. "Why, he could ruin his reputation being seen like this. Let me see if I can find my vinaigrette."

Mr. Jackson suggested that the good doctor might better be left to sleep it off, but Lady Blunder was obdurate. It was the least that she could do, she said, for someone who had saved her life so many times.

And she withdrew to a window to have more daylight with which to see inside her reticule. As she rummaged, Mr. Jackson drew Jenny aside. Everything about his face proclaimed honesty and earnestness, from the long line of his thick eyebrows to his broad chin. There was, in fact, something about his countenance that

Jenny found she liked more each time she saw him. This was someone to be depended on. No one who had seen him could ever doubt that. What a pity it was, she thought, that her aunt was using him for her own purposes.

"I am trying to understand your aunt," the coal merchant said solemnly. "Perhaps you can explain to me just why it is she should have chosen this gentleman to be her personal physician."

"My aunt sometimes sees things in the reverse," Jenny told him. "Besides, Dr. Dangle has any number of other clients who are quite able to overlook some of his bad habits in order to be prescribed to in any way they like. I mean to say, he is always ready to manufacture illnesses to order. And the medicines that he prescribes are harmless, on the whole."

She did not mention the night when Dr. Dangle had barely been prevented from operating on her uncle with his rusty instruments. How strange it was that her first impulse was to defend the doctor, but she was aware of an absurd sense of loyalty, not toward the doctor precisely, but certainly to her aunt. How odd that she could disapprove of her and her efforts to blacken Lady Carew's name on the one hand and, on the other, feel so defensive.

"I see," Mr. Jackson muttered, and perhaps, Jenny thought, he did. How fortunate her aunt could be if she would only take him seriously. Not many men would trouble themselves to try to understand her eccentric ways. Jenny could only hope that her aunt would see his value in the end, although her record for making accurate evaluations of character certainly was not reassuring.

Lady Blunder hurried back to them, confessing that she had forgotten her vinaigrette, apparently, and demanding their suggestion as to another restorative, Dr. Dangle remaining in his unconscious state. Mr. Jackson, to please her, suggested that mineral water be applied to the doctor's forehead and, further, that he would go in search of coffee, which he understood was frequently of value in such a case.

"No, no!" Lady Blunder cried. "I want you with me in case he should begin to slide off his chair. Jenny can fetch the coffee. There is a shop just on the corner. Have them put it in a jar, my dear. They will think it very odd, perhaps, but if you pay people they will do anything. At least that has been my experience. Oh, la, Mr. Jackson! Only look! It is just as I feared. He *is* about to slide!"

As Mr. Jackson and Lady Blunder rushed to put the doctor right, Jenny made her way out of the Pump Room with mixed feelings. She was willing enough to help Dr. Dangle, and she supposed that, given the circumstances, this was the only way to go about it. But she was afraid that her aunt would have no intention of letting the matter rest once he was sober. Clearly she was convinced that something had happened to him. How far would she decide to go in her role as Good Samaritan? Clearly it did not occur to her—or perhaps it did not matter—that she was drawing considerable attention. Jenny was aware that everyone in Bath, including her uncle, took her aunt for granted as a confirmed eccentric, but Jenny thought that she would like it better if the older woman could learn, somehow, not to be so easily deceived.

The narrow streets were thronged with passersby and carriages, and that in itself caused Jenny some delay. Then, at the coffee-house, it was difficult to convince the proprietor to give her coffee to take away for he declared that ale was one thing, since it was common for people to come to taverns with their pails, but coffee was quite another matter, and he would have to give it his consideration.

In the end, but only when Jenny had explained the precise nature of the difficulty, he agreed and filled a jug with coffee for which he demanded ample payment indeed. All in all considerable time had passed before Jenny made her return to the Pump Room, and there, while she was carefully making her way through the crowd and concentrating on keeping the coffee from spilling, Miss Williams made her confrontation.

"I wondered where you were, Miss Allen," she said, slim and confident in her stylish London morning gown of flowered brocade. "You really must do something about your aunt, you know.

She and that coalmonger are making a laughing stock of themselves with that drunken Dr. Dangle. I knew that I was right in telling Lady Lamont that if she wanted me to remain in her house she really must dismiss him."

"Let me help you with the jug, Miss Allen," Lord Lamont said and Jenny started, for she had not seen him at once.

"Ah, so you are bringing coffee," he said, taking it from her. "I suspect that is precisely what is needed. Come. Follow me, both of you."

Miss Williams followed, as did Jenny, but she did not put a cease to her harangue. Dr. Dangle should be in gaol. There was no telling how many people he had murdered.

"I cannot believe that anyone in their right mind would let him near them, let alone prescribe," she concluded as they approached the threesome in the corner.

Jenny bit her lip to keep from laughing, and, indeed, there was something funny about the sight of her aunt sitting next to Dr. Dangle on one side and Mr. Jackson on the other, both of them with their hands folded and their eyes staring straight ahead, as though to make it seem quite ordinary that the gentleman between them should let his head fall first on one shoulder and then the other, like some weary pendulum. As for Lord Lamont, she saw the familiar sardonic glint in his dark eyes as he took a glass from the counter where mineral water was dispersed, filled it with coffee from the jug and offered it to Mr. Jackson.

It was precisely the right thing to do, signifying, as it did, that the coal dealer was in charge of the situation. In a very few minutes Dr. Dangle had been forced to consume almost the full glass and, since it was steaming hot, he was scalded into consciousness.

"You ought to be ashamed of yourself, Sir!" Miss Williams exclaimed in her witty manner. "You have made a disgrace of yourself! Whatever little reputation that you ever had has been completely stripped away from you! Worse, you have made a scandal of a respectable profession. Lady Lamont is somewhere about, and I can only hope she has not seen you. If I were you, Lady Blunder, I would give him no more of your association. Someone like Mr. Jackson, who runs no risk to his reputation, can see the doctor home."

Jenny caught her breath. The implication of the last thing to be said was clear. Because Mr. Jackson was nothing but a coalmonger, he could be seen with the drunken doctor. She did not know whether that was worse than what had come before. The doctor, in his present state, was clearly in need of help, not defamation.

"I cannot believe that I have heard my ears!" Lady Blunder cried, rising from her chair in a ferocious manner. "How wrong I have been about you, Miss Williams. I thought you witty.

Took your comments to mean precisely the reverse, as is suitable to irony. But you have been speaking your mind all along."

"I never pretended otherwise, Madam," Miss Williams replied, raising her chin. "I could not think why, every time I spoke, you laughed, but now I understand. No, I am quite in earnest, Madam. This man is a disgrace. I had him turned out of Lady Lamont's house this morning. With her approval, I might add." ·

Jenny could not understand why Lord Lamont let her go on like this. His face was expressionless again, except for a shadow of a frown.

"No doubt that explains his present state!" Lady Blunder cried. "The poor man has been trying to forget his sorrows."

Dr. Dangle was looking about himself with an air of surprised discovery as though he had thought, on wakening, to find himself in his own bed. Instead a crowd had gathered, and Lady Blunder was eye to eye with the young lady who had given him his walking papers from Lady Lamont's.

"She did it to me!" the good doctor declared. "She had the butler show me to the door. A door which has been open to me these many years. Why, I counted Lady Lamont as more than a patient, 'struth I did. She was a friend of mine, despite the difference in our station."

And with that surprisingly coherent speech, he collapsed in tears. Jenny thought that although he might have seemed amusing a few minutes earlier when he was nodding like a pendulum between her aunt and Mr. Jackson, he was a truly pathetic figure now.

"I know you think us all absurd, Miss Williams," Lady Blunder was saying. "Perhaps we are. But you do not understand our ways, and you have made no attempt to try. Dr. Dangle serves a useful purpose to a few of us. He is quite right when he says he cares. Not that he is adverse to his fee. I would think the less of him if he were. But he coddles us and does not make us always feel we must be well. Why, the gentleman is so agreeable that he will take our word for whether we are sick or well, instead of pretending to be quite godlike, as some doctors do. And his medicines are so innocuous that we never have any fear of taking them. And surely he cannot help it if he is not always turned out as smartly as some of his fellows. After all, he is unmarried. And he has had a trying life. I have listened to a good many stories about it, Miss Williams, and I assure you..."

"Any doctor who would tell his patients stories about his own intimate affairs should be mistrusted, for a start," Miss Williams told her.

"I will not be interrupted by a chit of a girl like yourself!" Lady Blunder told her. "I have said the last words on the subject. Dr. Dangle may be in no fit condition now. If the truth be told, I might be willing to admit that this is not the first time I have seen him in something close

175

to this condition. But I will defend him, willy nilly, to the last. And now, Miss, if you would be so good as to move, Mr. Jackson and I will see that he is taken home in safety. You did a good day's work when you had him turned away from Lady Lamont's, and I hope you are quite satisfied with yourself."

chapter sixteen

Jenny did not see anything of Letty that evening.
The Assembly Rooms were as crowded as they
ever were, and it was only from a distance that
she saw Lady Carew attach herself, as she always did, to Sir Simon. The deed was done then!
Letty had started on elopement! And in a few
hours Lady Carew would discover that she had
lost her daughter. The thought of it made Jenny
feel so strange that she sat down at the side of
the octagonal entry room and told her aunt and
Mr. Jackson to go on without her.

"I always enjoy seeing people arrive," she
said, knowing that she needed no more than a
feeble excuse to send them on their way.

The morning's events had made a great
impression on Lady Blunder. Not only had the
veil been drawn from her eyes in the matter of

Miss Williams, but she was full of what appeared to be genuine admiration about the way in which Mr. Jackson had handled Dr. Dangle.

"I have never in my life seen such a masterful gentleman in an emergency," she had confided in Jenny that afternoon. "Not a word to my brother, mind, for he would tell Lady Carew, and there is nothing she would like better than to think that I find anything about him to like."

Jenny had wanted to argue with her aunt to the effect that she was deceiving herself about Lady Carew being Mr. Jackson's motivating genius, but, knowing she was not likely to be believed, she held her tongue.

"We took Dr. Dangle to his rooms in town," Lady Blunder had continued. "And such a dreadful state of things you truly cannot imagine. He told us that the arrangement was that the landlady would see to keeping everything tidy, but clearly she has taken advantage of his...his problem all along. Mr. Jackson said it was not to be endured, and so he took the doctor along with him to the house he has rented on the Royal Crescent. He said he wanted to be near me," she added wistfully. "And I pretended to believe it."

It appeared that Mr. Jackson was determined to change Dr. Dangle's ways, and when Jenny demanded what reason he had to do that for a total stranger, Lady Blunder flushed and said that, of course, he had told her that he would do the same for anyone she valued.

"But of course this is only part of the plot to impress me," she concluded. "To win my regard so that I will be even more bitterly disappointed later. Well, well, my dear, both he and Lady Carew will have their just reward. In the meantime I will give the gentleman his due. And as long as what he does is to Dr. Dangle's advantage, I will make no complaint."

She had then launched into the diatribe against Miss Williams and, indirectly, Lord Lamont, too.

"I cannot understand why he permits such rudeness from her!" she exclaimed. "I expected him to say something this morning. You know I think him lacking in compassion for his mother. But I have never charged him with anything more than selfishness. He is an admirable young gentleman in many ways, and I can well see why Miss Williams should want him as a prize. But Oliver has never been known for the long duration of his patience, and I expected him to cut her off before her attack became too outrageous. Why, it is as though the chit had taken over their household. I told Lady Lamont that myself. 'You must not allow that gel to make a footstool of you,' I said."

"You have spoken with Lady Lamont already?" Jenny asked her.

"As soon as Mr. Jackson was settled, I went directly to her," Lady Blunder replied. "She was just returning from the Pump Room, and Oliver and that frightful Miss Williams were with her.

Fortunately the gel went up to her room. If she had not, I would have made a point of speaking to Devina alone. But I did not mind Oliver being there. Indeed, I was glad of it, for no matter what he thinks of his Miss Williams, he might as well know that not all of us agree."

There was something magnificent about Lady Blunder when she was in a rage, or so Jenny had thought as she had watched her aunt stride back and forth across the sitting room until she made it seem that it was little more than a closet. Her anger filled the room and overflowed into the corridor. Sir Simon must have felt it, for Jenny saw him tiptoe past the door on his way up the stairs.

"Well, I told them that I had been insulted by that...that person," Lady Blunder had continued, rubbing her hands. "And I told dear Devina how Dr. Dangle had been libeled and that Oliver had stood by without a word. And I said that Devina must know she had been wrong to dismiss Dr. Dangle so abruptly and that she should not allow herself to be influenced by Miss Williams."

"And what was her response?" Jenny asked her.

"That is the strange part," Lady Blunder had replied, coming to a sudden halt before the settee where Jenny sat. "Devina is a woman of strong spirits. I mean to say she never lets herself be managed by anyone but Oliver. And she has always placed such great faith in Dr. Dangle that I know it must have been terrible for her to have let him go in such a way. But all that she would do was to stare at the carpet and say there was no help for it. And then she muttered something about his being a great fraud."

Lady Blunder assumed a murderous expression and arched her nose in quite a frightening manner. "I told her that of course he was a fraud. They are all frauds, doctors! Particularly here in Bath when they have so many patients at their disposal. But at least Dr. Dangle never pretended to be anything else but a charlatan, I told her. At least you knew precisely where you stood with him. He did not take a guinea from you and pretend to be doing you a favor. Whatever you might say about Dr. Dangle, he did not condescend."

"Did Lady Lamont agree?" Jenny asked her.

"She *said* I was entitled to my opinion!" Lady Blunder raged. "She *said* she had been persuaded that it would be best if she let him go. She *said* that Oliver had been warning her against him for years. I turned on him when she said that, but he only said that he had given no advice on the matter of whether Dr. Dangle should go or stay."

"It was entirely Miss Williams' decision, Lady Lamont told me, and when I challenged Devina on that—because I did, you know—and demanded to know if it were true that she was no longer mistress in her own house, she begged me to understand in quite an uncharacteristic fashion. She gave me no reason, mind you. And so I came away. But I am disappointed. Very. And when Miss Williams and Oliver marry, as it now seems clear they will, I can see no way that Devina and I can remain friends."

All this Jenny remembered as she sat looking at the fashionable crowds descending on the ballroom. How could she go on pretending that it did not matter to her that Lord Lamont meant to offer for the witty and beautiful Miss Mary Williams? She would make his life a misery. But that was not *her* concern. No more was her aunt's quarrel with Lady Carew. Or Letty's elopement. She felt, quite suddenly, as though she were in a foreign country, an observer of an exotic scene which she could never quite be part of. Bath offered excitement, clearly, but she did not know that she could ever find happiness here.

A young viscount she had danced with once before on a similar occasion asked her for the first cotillion, and Jenny took his arm as they made their way to the ballroom. She had met a good many attractive men in passing, but she had not cared enough about them even to remember their names. All that must change now, she told herself. It would not do to mope over Lord Lamont's engagement. And so she threw back her neck when they made their figures on the line and laughed a good deal in a charming fashion, and knew from the look in certain eyes that she was making an impression. But all she could think of was Miss Williams and Lord Lamont, and Letty and her captain who were even now on their way to Gretna Green.

She decided that she envied Letty. Awful as it was to be forced to deceive a mother, it must be so exciting to make an elopement. The moon was shining tonight and it was mild. They would be sitting close together in his carriage and smiling into one another's eyes. They would be..."

"Your thoughts must be extraordinarily engrossing, Miss Allen," someone said and, looking up, she saw Lord Lamont beside her. The viscount had been succeeded by a knight who had been succeeded by the third son of an earl who was even now fetching her some punch. Waiting, she had fallen into her daydream, not expecting that Lord Lamont would be the one to waken her from it.

"I could not tell whether your thoughts were pleasant or the contrary," he said. "You often wear a mixed expression."

He had noticed? But, of course, he had already told her that something about her wakened his curiosity.

"I came to ask you to take the next dance with me," he said. "It is a gavotte, I believe."

"But what about Miss Williams?" Jenny exclaimed before she thought that it might have been more delicate not to.

"Gavottes are too vigorous for Miss Williams, I believe," he told her with a smile. "She is tell-

183

ing my mother something of its history now, I think. Something about it being danced by French peasants originally. Miss Williams does not like to think in terms of peasants. More particularly, she does not care to dance like them."

Was there a tiny tinge of mockery in his voice, or was he simply telling her the truth? Jenny glanced at where Miss Williams was standing beside Lady Lamont's chair and saw that she was not telling her a story now, at any rate. Indeed, Miss Williams looked grim, and Lady Lamont appeared to be in a state of extreme agitation by the flutter of her hands. Given the circumstances and considering Lord Lamont's pending engagement to Miss Williams, it was surely odd of him to ask her to dance, Jenny thought. Could there have been some disagreement between him and Miss Williams? Was this his way of getting his revenge?

"Why are you asking me to take the floor with you, Sir?" Jenny asked him, at the same time wondering why on earth it was that when she was with him she suffered such irresistible impulses to be frank. She had just asked the most gauche sort of question, which, no doubt, would go far to reinforce his opinion of her. Just as she had thought it might, the question made him smile.

"Do you know, Miss Allen," he replied, "that is a question I never have been asked before. You really are an original, you know. I am asking you to dance because I would like to dance with you. Allow me to apologize for not being able to come up with a more clever reason."

At that moment the third son of an earl, who had been fetching Jenny punch, appeared, and there were a few awkward moments while she explained that she meant to dance the next dance with Lord Lamont. And dance they did. Jenny whirled about until her cheeks were glowing and her black curls were tangled. Both of them finished, breathless, hand in hand.

They were laughing when the music stopped, but laughter turned to silence. Jenny's fingers were released. She took two steps away from him but did not leave.

"Will you tell me what was troubling you before?" he asked her, as simply as though they had known one another for a long time. The people pressing all around them seemed to fade away as though a giant hand had pressed an eraser to them. To Jenny it was as though they were as much alone as they had been in the mist-shrouded carriage.

"What would you do," she asked him, giving in to her desire to confide, "if a friend were breaking with a parent in the most serious of ways? What would you do if this same friend were doing something which would cause a good deal of heartbreak and anxiety? What would you do if you were the only one to know the secret?"

"You feel this friend has not been wise?" he asked her.

"She says she will be happy," Jenny said, coming as close to the truth as she dared without revealing Letty's plan. "She is taking steps which seem necessary."

"Can she be dissuaded or stopped?" Lord Lamont asked her, his dark eyes narrowed as he gave her his full attention.

"Neither," Jenny told him. "It is too late for that."

"What can be done then?" he asked her gently. "That is what is troubling you, I assume."

Jenny was grateful to him for not pressing her for particulars. Further, everything he was saying was calculated to make her feel less guilty.

"I feel I should have advised her," she murmured. "Asked her to take more time to think, at any rate. And now I feel—well, that her mother should know at once. Be warned. Even though she can do no more to stop it than she can when this ball ends."

"Is that when she will find out?" Lord Lamont asked her. And, when Jenny nodded: "In my opinion you should let matters take their course. Unless your friend has put herself in danger. I take it that is not the case."

"She has assured me that she will be quite safe, and I believe her," Jenny replied, dropping her glance because she did not want him to think...

"Did you promise to keep the secret?" he murmured.

"She did not ask me precisely to promise to keep the secret, but I know that she believes I will."

"Then I repeat what I said before," the young marquess told her. "If speaking out will do no good, say nothing. And remember this. All of us must take on the consequences of our actions. It will amuse you to hear me moralizing, no doubt, but I have had occasion to think along those lines just recently. Sometimes it would seem easiest to step in and order the affairs of others. Exert whatever power you may have. Flatly explain that this, that and the other is true. But often it is more effective by far to let them make their own decisions, and by decisions, in this case, I mean mistakes. Once they pay the consequences, they will be wiser by far. The important thing is not to blame yourself."

The third son of an earl appeared that moment to ask for another dance. Lord Lamont bowed and returned to his mother and Miss Williams, leaving Jenny feeling dazed by such a rapid transition back to the present. And, although she smiled at the young gentleman beside her, her mind was far away.

chapter seventeen

*Throughout that fateful evening, Jenny never for
a moment forgot Lady Carew and often saw her,
usually on Sir Simon's arm. Jenny had always
liked her. Certainly she had never failed to be
kind. There was that strange, girlish quality
about her which manifested itself in her manner
with her daughter. This evening, knowing what
was soon to happen, Jenny was aware of a new
vulnerability which seemed to surround her
like an aura. She had trusted Letty so. Would
she ever be able to trust her again?*

Jenny was glad that she had confided in Lord
Lamont. Otherwise, she might have yielded to
impulse and gone to Lady Carew to try to prepare her, at least, for the shock which so soon
should follow. Her secret was like a heavy
weight inside her but she did not let any of her

dancing partners guess that she was anything other than the laughing beauty whose feet were so very light.

Rarely did Jenny's thoughts concern themselves with these young men that evening, although she charmed them with her eyes. She thought of Letty and wondered whether she was happily pressed against her lover as their carriage sped through the night. Or was she weeping out her guilt because the most important moments of her life must be hidden away in secret as though what she was doing were a crime.

The last dance was a quadrille, which was stately enough, apparently, to satisfy Miss Williams' requirements, for she took the floor with Lord Lamont, a proud figure in her scarlet gown with her beautiful fair hair piled high on her head and caught with scarlet ribbons. Further down the line with the persistent third son of an earl as her partner, Jenny watched Miss Williams move through the figures with so much grace that she seemed to turn her dancing to an art. She did not often smile, however, perhaps because she was concentrating so on every movement. Now and then, however, Jenny saw a particular way she looked at Lord Lamont, as though there was a secret between them. No doubt, Jenny told herself, it would not be long before a notice of the engagement would appear in all the papers.

As for herself, Jenny thought that she could

see that the round of entertainment which Bath provided might be the key. It would be simple to maintain such a constant round of activity that one would never know whether one were happy or not. Yes, of course! That would be the perfect solution. And someday, no doubt, when she least expected it, someone would come along and...

But she did not really think he would. No more, no doubt, had Letty when she had tried to do without her captain. But at least Letty had had a choice. There was nothing to prevent her from telling him her love was too strong to let them stay apart. Jenny's position was very difficult. If Lord Lamont thought of her at all it was as an amusing figure whom he thought of as a sister. He liked her. That much was clear. He would never have asked her what was troubling her if he had not cared for her happiness. And that would have to do.

The quadrille had just come to an end, and Jenny's partner was just returning her to Lady Blunder when Lady Carew screamed. Turning so quickly that her gown billowed about her, Jenny hurried in the direction of the sound, realizing that she had been half expecting it all evening. Squeezing past a cluster of curious, old women, she saw Lady Carew holding a piece of paper and knew that it must be Letty's letter. Lady Carew's other hand was pressed to her mouth, as though the sharp cry had been ripped from her without permission. Sir Simon stood behind her, one hand on her arm, and Jenny saw that his eyes were squinted in an effort to make out the words.

"'Sdeath!" Jenny heard him exclaim and, in a moment, he had hurried Lady Carew to a corner of the room where they could be less public, and it was there that Jenny joined them with Lady Blunder, together with Mr. Jackson, close behind.

"What on earth has happened?" Lady Blunder demanded. "Tell me, Simon. Is she ill? I think she must be, for she has gone quite pale."

And, bringing out her ubiquitous vinaigrette, she waved it under Lady Carew's nose.

"No, no!" the lady told her, pushing the vinaigrette away. "I am in no likelihood of fainting, Lady Blunder. The fact is that I have received shocking news."

"Is someone dead?" Lady Blunder demanded. "Has there been a tragedy?"

"Her daughter, Letty, has eloped," Sir Simon said quietly. "Perhaps you will recall Captain Walker who was in Bath a while ago. They are on their way to Gretna Green this instant. In fact, they have been gone several hours already."

The ancient enmity which Lady Blunder had for Lady Carew on account of the latter having won her brother's affections was swept away in an instant. It would have been easy for her to have reminded Lady Carew that, had she made it a practice to keep her eyes closer pinned on

Letty, this never would have happened. Indeed, there were any number of stinging things which must have come to mind. But she swept them away and embraced the other woman, and, when she had finished, Jenny did the same.

"Did you know of this betimes, my dear," Lady Carew asked her.

It was a question Jenny had not expected. And yet she answered it without any hesitation. And truthfully.

"And did it not occur to you to tell me?" Lady Carew pressed her. She had shed no tears yet, but she was trembling with the effort to suppress them, and Lady Blunder had her arm about her.

Despite the fact that they had removed themselves to a corner, there was a little press about them, and people on their way to the doors tended to pause for a few minutes to listen and then tell others. Indeed, the ballroom was as full of buzzing sounds as though the company were bees.

"No doubt Letty swore her to secrecy," she heard her uncle say in his usual mild manner. "Besides, if Letty was determined to elope, she would have found some other way had this one been prevented."

"I only want to know why you did not tell me, Jenny," Lady Carew said, speaking as though her lips were stiff. "Is your uncle right. Was it a sworn secret?"

"Not precisely," Jenny told her. "But she expected me to treat it as a confidence. Even so, it crossed my mind…"

She broke off, seeing that Lord Lamont was standing close by with his mother on one hand and Miss Williams on the other.

"Miss Allen consulted me," he said, so unexpectedly that Jenny started and raised her fingers to her cheek. "It was my opinion that, particularly since the elopement was in process, she should respect your daughter's wishes, Madam."

"You approved of an elopement?" Miss Williams was heard demanding. "You countenanced such a thing? Why, you amaze me, Sir. Indeed you do!"

If Lord Lamont answered, Jenny did not hear him, for Lady Carew was speaking, and this time her voice was rising sharply, as though hysteria threatened.

"I can forgive Letty anything except that she did not trust me!" she cried. "To do this behind my back! To come here with me this evening, pretending…Secret letters. Secret plans. So many things kept from me! And all the time I liked to think of us as sisters. I told her everything, or nearly. And she…and she betrayed me!"

It was so exactly what Jenny had feared would happen that tears rose in her eyes. "She only wants to make you understand that she really loves him," Jenny said in a low voice. "She loves him enough to suffer the consequences of his bravery—if there are any consequences. You cannot be sure of that."

"Tell me," Jenny heard Mr. Jackson ask her aunt under the cover of his hand, "is this chap respectable?"

"Very," Lady Blunder replied, while everyone near her strained to hear. As though to gratify their curiosity, she raised her voice. "Miss Carew has eloped with a captain in His Majesty's army."

Seeing that her audience was attentive, she gave over all pretense of informing Mr. Jackson privately and made a general announcement to the effect that Captain Walker was a gallant gentleman who had just returned from Yorktown where, despite the fact that victory had gone to the Americans, he had distinguished himself time and time again.

"And has the medals to show for it!" she declared as a grand conclusion.

There was a general outcry from the crowd at that to know just why, if what Lady Blunder said was true, it had been necessary for an elopement, and Miss Williams was overheard to say something tart about tempests in teapots.

"Lady Carew is afraid that, if there is another war and—given governments and men in general, there are sure to be—Captain Walker will take a risk too many and her daughter will be left a widow," Lady Blunder said, demonstrating that she was singularly well informed.

"Why, as for that," someone in the crowd replied, "any gentleman among us might be run down by a horse as we cross the public way. Which does not mean, I hope sincerely, that no one should marry us."

"It is not the same thing," Lady Blunder replied. "It is not the same thing at all!"

Jenny was quite certain that Lady Carew would prefer that her most private affairs not be debated publicly like this. But the fact was that she did not seem to care, or did not notice, either way, for she had turned aside a bit and Sir Simon was talking to her urgently.

"A gentleman who puts himself in danger at every opportunity does not deserve domestic pleasures," a voice said clearly, and Jenny, turning, saw that Miss Williams, while making her progress toward the door, had cast this parting arrow. The certainty with which she spoke, together with the lack of passion, made Jenny flush with anger. But before she could so much as speak, Miss Williams added: "And any young lady silly enough to run away to Gretna Green does not deserve much sympathy. It is such a provincial thing to do."

This last was added with a disdain so strong that many people turned to stare at her, and even Lady Lamont was seen to raise her eyebrows. As for Lord Lamont, he had wiped his face of all expression. Certainly there was nothing about him to make Jenny think that he disapproved of what Miss Williams had said. What a strange man he was. Above all, not consistent. But that was beside the point. If he was not willing to rebuke Miss Williams, Jenny was.

"If by provincial, you mean grounded in honest emotion instead of sterility of feeling, then no doubt that is true," she said defiantly.

Miss Williams stopped in her traces and stared at Jenny in a particular way which made it clear she condescended.

"How strange you are, Miss Allen," she declared sharply. "Always doing and saying the oddest things. Pulling Lord Lamont off to introduce a man he had never met to your aunt—and a coal dealer, too! And other things I will not mention, as though Lord Lamont were not well accustomed to girlish intrigues and how to avoid them. And now you pretend to define provincialism to me.... La, it is too absurd. Come, Lady Lamont. It is getting late."

"I think there is something in what the gel has said," the older woman by her side declared. "I liked that bit about sterility of feeling. It gave the words to something which has been troubling me of late."

"Yes, Miss Allen," Lord Lamont said, apparently quite seriously. "Given head or heart to follow, which would you choose? In a word, do you think your friend acted correctly?"

Jenny was aware that even Lady Carew was listening now, and she chose her words with care. "I think that if she and Captain Walker love one another, then they should marry," she said. "She owed it to her mother to consult her.

If there had been some objection with which she could agree, perhaps.... But no. She loves him. In the end, that rules out every argument. And yet it pained her...."

Lady Carew came forward to take her hand. "She did not want to hurt me?" she said.

"She would have done anything to prevent it," Jenny said in a low voice. "You must believe me. Anything but give the captain up. Can you forgive her for that?"

For a moment the older woman simply looked at Jenny, and, for the first time, the girl saw the tiny lines which, deepened only slightly, would make her seem her age. She hoped that what Letty had done would not make that happen.

"You have represented my daughter loyally," she murmured.

"I have only said what I believe," Jenny replied. "You must understand how much pain it gave her to deceive you and how much she hopes that you will see that she was right in the end."

Lady Carew raised a hand and smoothed a dark curl back from Jenny's forehead. Her eyes looked into a distance Jenny could not see.

"When Letty's father died, it was so dreadful for me," the older woman said. "Now and then the wound will tingle still. When I thought of the possibility of my own daughter suffering that pain...And with the captain it was more likely that she might be widowed. But I should have known.... Love does not make these considerations."

"Why then, it should," Miss Williams was heard to say, but Lady Carew did not pay her any heed. Her attention was focused on Jenny now.

"I can forgive Letty anything," she told the girl. "As long as she is safe and happy I will never again intrude with my advice."

"I think you have made the right decision," Lady Blunder declared, approaching her old enemy with a smile. "You are a remarkable woman in some ways, Lady Carew, and I do not care who hears me say it."

And, just as they embraced, a familiar voice was heard over the buzz of all the others, and Jenny turned toward the door to see Letty and a fair young man in uniform come hurrying into the room.

"Mama!" the girl cried, running toward Lady Carew with arms spread wide. "David and I decided that we *would* have your blessing. We drove a ways and then we knew that was wrong. Mind you, we will not be separated. You *must* agree!"

"I know I must, my dear," Lady Carew said with a smile, stretching one hand out to the captain. "You and your husband-to-be must know that I have tried to be too sensible by far."

"There is no such thing as too much sense," Miss Williams observed, as she swept out of the ballroom, taking Lady Lamont with her and with the young marquess following behind. And if his smile was sardonic, Jenny was too far away to tell. But, as she told herself, it did not matter. Letty, at least, was happy, and she could always warm herself in her dear friend's glow. If something inside her fought to play the rebel, then she would put it down.

chapter eighteen

It was always possible to tell Lady Blunder's mood from the condition of a huge fern which stood in the window of the sitting room. When she was happy, its mistress lavished attention upon it, watering it fondly, humming a little tune and puffing its leaves with particular tenderness. In recent days, because of her conviction that Mr. Jackson was Lady Carew's agent, she had all but ignored the plant, however, and it had begun to languish in a distressing way. On the morning following the dramatic ending to the ball at the Assembly Rooms, however, Jenny found her aunt lavishing fond attention on the plant, watering can close at hand.

"What a delightful morning!" Lady Blunder declared, apparently determined to ignore the overcast quality of the day. "I have had a note from Lady Lamont. She means to pay us a morning visit, together with Miss Williams and Oliver. She said she had a most particular business to discuss, and I would not be at all surprised if she means to ask my advice about the engagement party. She mentions something about a picnic in the gardens across the river. Now that would be unique!"

Jenny stared out a window and noted how low the clouds hung over the river. How could she ever have found Bath to be an exciting town, she wondered. And Lady Lamont was to visit! She had been relieved when she had heard that her aunt had decided not to attend the Pump Room this morning. The view from her bedroom window was the same as the one she looked at now, nothing but the great, gaping mouth of the Circus, and the cobbled alley which was Gay Street, leading dankly down to the center of the city, which was certain to be jammed, as always, with sedan chairs. The same people making the same pilgrimages to the baths. The same chatter in the Pump Room. Oh, the awful, gray sameness of it all!

"My dear!" Lady Blunder declared, oblivious of her niece's depression. "I cannot tell you what a relief it is to have opened my heart to dear Elaine!"

For a moment Jenny could not think who it was her aunt referred to, and then she remembered that was Lady Carew's name. Her mood improved for a moment when she remembered how Letty had gone off the night before, arm in arm with both her mother and Captain Walker. But then she remembered how Miss Williams had sniffed at all of the proceedings and how Lord Lamont had shown no disapproval of her attitude, and her dejection returned in an instant.

"What a lovely fern you are!" Lady Blunder crooned. "Poor dear, you have been so lonely. A little fluff just here and there will make all the difference. And here's another lovely drink."

Jenny felt a sense of claustrophobia settle over her. How did it happen that this house, this town, could seem to become a prison? She knew she must do something to change her mood, but she could think of nothing. And yet to consider months of this endless social round... And Lord Lamont gone. Married to the beautiful and witty Miss Williams.

"How wrong it was of me," Lady Blunder continued, pursuing her own thoughts, "to ever have suspected her of having arranged for Mr. Jackson to meet me to further her own ends. As I told Simon, he should have told me how wrongheaded I was being. And, as for Mr. Jackson being a coal dealer, I hope I am no snob. He carries himself like a gentleman and that is the great thing, don't you agree?"

Jenny thought that probably the thing which recommended Mr. Jackson most to her aunt, although she would not admit it, was his obvious and absolute devotion to her. Whenever he was in her presence, as at the ball the night before, he followed her about with such a contented expression on his broad, ruddy face that Jenny had to look away in order not to feel a certain sadness, knowing as she did that her aunt was using him to make her case against Lady Carew. But now, apparently, all that had changed. Jenny knew that she should care, feel some delight, both for her uncle's and her aunt's sake. Now, presumably, Sir Simon would feel free to offer for Lady Carew. All would end happily for everyone. And she *was* happy, or would be if it was not that she felt nothing.

"He has worked miracles for Dr. Dangle," Lady Blunder went on, still absorbed in thoughts of Mr. Jackson, meanwhile continuing to poke and pat the fern in just the manner which would give it the most satisfaction. "Yes, the dear doctor intends to make his debut in public soon, and Mr. Jackson assures me that everyone will be amazed. And when I tell him that I must confess to liking Dr. Dangle the way he was, Mr. Jackson will insist on teasing me and saying that I must wait and see."

And on she rattled about subjects as diverse as the fascinating things that Mr. Jackson had told her about coal and her opinion of Miss Williams.

"I confess to being disappointed with dear Devina," she declared. "No doubt she thinks that she has chosen wisely, but I think the gel lacks feeling. But I intend to say nothing. Nothing! I have always made a point of letting others make their own mistakes, and I will continue as I began. La, my dear! The time! They will be here at any moment, and I must have Dorothy attend to my hair. In the meantime, you will be doing me a favor if you will sit down at the pianoforte and play this dear plant a tune or two. I assure you, it will make all the difference."

Jenny thought that she would be willing to do anything to stop her aunt from chattering. But what a temptation to slip out the door and into the gray morning. To be away from here when Lady Lamont and the two others—she *would* not think of them in any other way—arrived. However, her aunt would wonder if she did not hear her play. And so Jenny sat down at the pianoforte and spread her lilac, muslin skirts around her and began to play first quite at random, tunes snatched from here and there, and then some music she had written for her own pleasure to match the poem by Andrew Marvell which she liked the best, "The Definition of Love."

> My Love is of a birth as rare
> As 'tis, for object, strange and high:
> It was begotten by Despair
> Upon Impossibility.

How strange it was, she told herself, as her fingers roamed the keys to make a lyric pause between the stanzas, that those words she had first read as a girl in the schoolroom should be so true today.

> And yet I quickly might arrive
> Where my extended soul is fixed:
> For Fate does iron wedges drive,
> And always crowds itself betwixt.

Even in the most ordinary of times, Jenny played with feeling, but now it was as though her emotions were pouring from her fingertips, and the rising music broke like a storm over the silent household. Down in the kitchen, Cook stopped stirring her pudding and cocked her head to listen, while upstairs in his chamber Sir Simon, tying his cravat, told himself that his niece had hidden depths.

> Unless the giddy heaven fall,
> And earth some new convulsion tear,
> And, us to join, the world should all
> Be cramped into a planisphere.

So richly did the music flow that Jenny did not hear the knocker on the door, and her position in relation to the hall was such that she could not see the footman hurrying to open it. As Lord Lamont and his mother and Miss Williams came into the house, Jenny sang the final stanza, all unknowing that she was overheard.

Therefore the love which us doth bind,
But Fate so enviously debars,
Is the conjunction of the mind.
And opposition of the stars.

"How lovely, my dear," Lady Lamont said as
she came into the room, leaning on the cane
which she sometimes affected. "I am very fond
of Marvell. Very! Tell me, who wrote the tune?"

Jenny rose slowly from the stool, her hands
still lingering on the keys, although the song
was finished. "I did not hear you come in," she
began, knowing that she was flushing and hating it. How cool Miss Williams looked in her
brown and white walking dress with all the lace
about her elegant, long throat. Jenny realized
that she had been so busy brooding ever since
her aunt had told her they were to have company that she had not bothered to change into
something more appealing than the simple blue
and white striped gown which had been part of
the meager wardrobe she had brought with her.
And, like her aunt, she should have attended
to her hair which was simply tucked under a
lace-trimmed mob cap.

"We apologize for startling you," Lord Lamont said quietly. The hour was past ten and
he was in his riding costume. But no doubt the
daily exercise, which he had insisted on hereto-
fore, had given way to more important demands.

"It is remarkable how often young ladies

manage to be 'startled' in circumstances which compliment them," Miss Williams declared, pulling off her gloves and looking around the room in a manner which indicated that all this was a tiresome ordeal.

Jenny knew her cheeks were burning now. Miss Williams managed to use everything she did as proof that she was trying to attract Lord Lamont's attentions like so many others had tried in the past. How unfair she was, for, having won him, she could have had some generosity. At least, Jenny thought, she had the satisfaction of knowing that, despite the prestige of Miss Williams' teacher, she herself was the better player.

"The tune is mine, Madam," she said to Lady Lamont, ignoring Miss Williams' remark. "I am glad if you liked it."

"Why, it was perfectly delightful!" Lady Lamont assured her. "How naughty of you to keep your talents a secret, my dear. You should have been performing at Lady Madrigal's musical evenings long ago. I assure you, you would be quite the star."

Miss Williams did not take this well. She took the chair Jenny offered, and Lady Lamont arranged herself on the settee. And, while the latter chattered, Miss Williams looked increasingly grim. As for Lord Lamont, he did not seem to notice that anything was wrong and stood beside the fireplace, with one arm on the mantel, listening to his mother go on about how

much she had liked the piece, with Miss Wil
liams becoming grimmer every moment.

Lady Blunder's entry provided a welcome distraction until she began to speak with glowing praises about the rehabilitation of Dr. Dangle which Mr. Jackson had accomplished.

"For a coal merchant, he is very versatile indeed," Miss Williams interposed when Lady Lamont had finished expressing her fervent desire that the doctor be returned to them "restored" as soon as possible.

Lady Blunder flushed, but she was in such good temper that she could easily control herself, although she did turn her back on Miss Williams, which was not as simple a feat as it sounds since they were sitting on the same settee. Whereupon Miss Williams, in order not to feel ignored, set herself to making a conversation with Jenny, while Lord Lamont listened. Jenny could not understand why it was that, although he was not smiling, that old sardonic glint should have returned to his dark eyes.

"I expect you were thrilled by last night's events," she said in her peculiarly unpleasant way. "Miss Carew is your dearest friend, I take it. Girls together. Secrets. All that sort of thing."

Jenny decided to cure Miss Williams with her own medicine, if she were able.

"So that is what is meant by friendship in London circles," she replied. "How very glad I am to know. You sit in corners, do you, and whisper secrets?"

"I have never in my life done anything of the sort!" Miss Williams declared, clearly stung.

"Ah, then you have no friends," Jenny replied. "I am very sorry for it, but I confess that I am not at all surprised."

Lord Lamont made a sudden movement at that moment, and when Jenny turned to look at him she found that he had wandered to the window overlooking Bath, not far enough away not to overhear the conversation, but with his back turned to the two girls. No doubt he would think her petty and find her irony objectionable, Jenny told herself, but she had had quite enough of the witty and beautiful Miss Mary Williams and meant to put her down, once and for all.

"I have all the friends that I require, Miss Allen," the other said. She was wearing a Windsor hat with a half-veil which helped to hide her eyes, but Jenny was sitting near enough to know that they were sparkling with rage.

"I believe that a picnic in the gardens would be just the proper atmosphere," Lady Lamont was saying, and Jenny's heart sank as she remembered why this visit was taking place. How childish of her to try to raise her spirits by insulting Miss Williams. The old phrase about sticks and stones came to mind. Ah, well! No doubt she would do no lasting injury, but she would, at least, give herself *some* satisfaction.

"Where do you learn to play the pianoforte so nicely?" Miss Williams said, indicating by her tone that she might have said the same thing to a clever child. "And you write music, too. Or *say* you do. Frankly, I thought I found that refrain familiar, although I cannot remember where I have heard it before."

Jenny started to count ten before she answered, and when she reached eight Miss Williams went on.

"But, of course, I quite forget, you have a fortune," she said in a voice which was so shrill that the older women stopped their conversation to listen. "You must have had all of the finest teachers. All of them who care to live in the wilds of England, that is."

This time Jenny did not bother with counting. "Yorkshire is scarcely the wilderness I hear London to be," she said. "Certainly, if you are any proof, Miss Williams, the city creates a certain savagery I have never noticed in the North. As for my fortune, I haven't any. If you have heard otherwise, then you have been misled."

Miss Williams smiled in the mode of one about to deliver a *coup de grâce*. "I am not the only person to be misled," she said, with stress on the last word to make her meaning clear. "Mr. Basset—the Honorable Thomas Basset— firmly believes you have a fortune. And he is not the only one. He had it from your aunt, you see. You are not going to sit there, surely, and ask me to believe that you have nothing to do with *that!*"

"That was *my* folly, Miss Williams," Lady

Blunder said, rising in a stately manner which Jenny had never seen her assume before. "My niece protested, but the rumor was spread before she even arrived. Now, would you care to comment further?"

"I do not think *I* wish to hear Miss Williams comment on anything again," Lady Lamont declared, snapping her fan together in an angry sort of way. "Besides, she is returning home with me this instant to make the necessary preparations for her immediate return to her parents in London."

"But Lady Lamont..." Miss Williams exclaimed with a look of shocked astonishment on her classically molded face.

"I hope you will allow me to apologize for my guest," Lady Lamont said, nodding first to Jenny and then Lady Blunder. "I have put up with a good deal from her myself because I thought she would be ideal for Oliver, but I see now I was mistaken."

"Really!" Miss Williams cried, shooting out of her chair like an arrow. "I cannot believe that I am hearing this!"

"You should have heard it much earlier," Lady Lamont told her grimly. "You should have heard it when you were a good deal younger than you are today. Whoever led you to believe that you must be the final judge of everything and everyone? Whoever gave you the idea that you could regulate other people's lives?"

Jenny thought to glance at Lord Lamont and

211

saw that he was watching his mother closely with a strange look in his eyes. Would he go to Miss Williams presently and usher her from the room? Surely he did not intend to allow her to be spoken to in this manner, no matter if the speaker was his mother.

"Surely you did not expect me to stand by and see you administered to by a drunken quack?" Miss Williams demanded, flying to her own defense. "And when I told you that you should ignore his diagnosis and stop behaving as though you were ill when you were not, I did it for your own good, Madam. It is something your son should have done long ago."

"Oliver is not to blame in this!" Lady Blunder interrupted. "I have wronged him in the past, and I want to say quite publicly that he has taken the proper path. He made no attempt to pretend that he believed in all his mother's illnesses, and he did protest against Dr. Dangle. But never did he attempt to blackmail her to change her ways. The game between them was always played quite fairly because they both knew the rules."

"Rules!" Miss Williams cried. "You dare to speak to me of rules! And, as for blackmail, whatever is effective should be used. I simply said that I could not remain in the house with someone who always fancied themselves ill. And you saw yourself how quickly Lady Lamont responded."

"And if you think I have felt the better for it,

you are quite wrong," her hostess declared, punctuating her point by striking her cane against the floor. "I have allowed you to disturb the rhythm of my life because I thought that you would be able to tempt my son to settle down. And for a while I thought I had succeeded. But you have been too clever for me this time, Oliver."

"Too clever!" Miss Williams exclaimed. "What on earth do you mean, Madam."

"I thought because he did not make his excuses and go back to the estate as soon as I was better that you intrigued him," Lady Lamont told the girl. "But this time he decided to turn the tables on me. And it took me until today to realize it. But he and I will discuss that later."

"I want to hear!" Miss Williams demanded. "Has there been a general scheme to discredit me? Is that what you mean? Because, if you do, I can quite easily point my finger at the person responsible for it."

And she looked so meaningfully at Jenny that there was no mistaking her implication.

"If you think that I have slandered you," Jenny told her boldly, "you are quite wrong, I assure you."

"There was no need for anyone to slander Miss Williams," Lady Lamont retorted. "Every time she opens her mouth she slanders herself. That is blunt talk, my girl, but the shock may improve you. Nothing in Bath is good enough for you. You even mock the scenery, not to mention my best friends. If *we* enjoy Lady Madrigal's musical evenings, our right to do so should be respected."

"It was all that I could do to keep from laughing," Miss Williams told them. "Your little circle of friends, Madam, are absurdities, one and all!"

A little silence followed this declaration, and then, her face quite pale, Miss Williams turned and hurried from the room.

"This is the first time I was ever rude to a guest," Lady Lamont admitted. "But I felt that I must speak out."

"And quite right, too," Lady Blunder said. "Shall I come with you to see her on her way? There is a London coach leaving from the White Hart in about an hour."

"Will you come with us, Oliver?" Lady Lamont demanded. "Or do I guess correctly that you prefer to remain here?"

"The thought had crossed my mind, I confess," Lord Lamont told her with a slow smile. "If, that is, I have your permission, Lady Blunder."

"Perhaps you should ask my niece, Sir," Lady Blunder replied.

"If there is any objection," Jenny said, "I cannot think of it immediately. Stay, Sir, by all means. I would be glad of the company."

And yet she found, once the door was closed, that she was not quite as calm as she had sounded, not quite as composed as, no doubt, Miss Williams would have been in the same situation. She was aware of being with Lord Lamont in an atmosphere of intimacy. Perhaps it was the darkness of the day outside which put her in mind of that misty morning when he and she had sat together in his carriage. They were not as close together, granted, but that could soon be remedied.

The same thought must have crossed Lord Lamont's mind, for, in a moment, they were closer than they had ever been before. And Lady Blunder, following her friend out the front door, thought that she heard the sound of laughter.

chapter nineteen

The sun beamed broadly down on the Spring Garden on the day of Lady Lamont's picnic, which she was giving despite Miss Williams' departure, and, more particularly, because her son was finally affianced.

"I cannot think of anything more suitable," she had told Jenny on the day she had been told the news. "Dear Tabitha is my best friend and this will make us some sort of relations. Besides, you are quite perfect for dear Oliver in every way. I should have trusted him to make his own choice in the end."

Jenny thought he had been clever in thwarting Lady Lamont's plans to have him marry the witty, beautiful Miss Williams the way he had.

"This time I decided to break the pattern," Oliver had told her on the very day Miss Williams had been vanquished. "I cannot count the number of times my mother has seen to it that I was informed that she was severely ill with the result that I arrive in Bath to find some young lady of her choosing as a house guest. This time Miss Williams arrived after me instead of before. That was the only difference."

Jenny had felt his arms tighten about her, and she thought that she had never been so happy before.

"In the past," he continued, "I waited for my mother to show some sign of recovery and then returned to the country, straight away. I hope that you will like Upton Hall. It was originally a Tudor manor and..."

There had followed a description which had turned into more private talk, and half an hour had elapsed before they had returned to the strategy which he had employed to convince his mother to stop interfering in his private affairs.

"Miss Williams was so precisely the sort of person my mother does not like that I thought I might surprise her by remaining here in Bath just to let her have a chance to know the young lady better and come to wish she had not tried to foist her on me. And that is precisely what occurred."

"I thought that love had blinded you," Jenny had confessed. "To her worst faults, that is. And, after all, she was witty and beautiful."

"Was she indeed?" Oliver had asked her. "I must confess I never noticed. From the first day that I saw you—Dr. Dangle was taking your pulse by listening to your wrist, you will remember—I have thought of no other person but you. Which made it all the more difficult to pretend to take Miss Williams seriously."

"Do you remember that morning in the mist?" Jenny had asked him. "That was when I was really certain."

Once again they drifted into such a private talk as will not bear public repeating. And now, in honor of their engagement, musicians had been installed on a platform banked with flowers, tables were piled high with creams and jellies and numerous other delicacies and the guests were beginning to arrive, some having been rowed across the river and others having come by the bridge in carriages.

"Damme, my dear!" Sir Roger Ramsdale declared as he reached the informal reception line and had bowed his way past Lady Lamont and Lady Blunder. "You've made the catch of the season, and here were we all thinking that young lady down from London meant to carry him away. Lamont, my friend! You have my congratulations. The lass is a fine fresh beauty, even though I hear she comes to you quite dowryless. Hello there, Blunder! Glad to see you! And Lady Carew! Charming, as usual. I wouldn't be surprised if we were hearing another announcement soon. Eh? Eh?"

And off he swaggered to one of the refreshment tables, apparently convinced that he had satisfied all the demands of this particular social situation and quite prepared now to take his enjoyment where he could find it.

In the pause which followed, Jenny and Oliver exchanged a smile, and the look in his dark eyes was as far from being sardonic as anything could be. And, indeed, she was a picture in a blue and white brocaded gown with her black curls caught up with matching ribbons and a glow on her face which only happiness can bring.

Sir Timity and Mr. Basset were the next ones to arrive. The Honorable Tommy, without his castanets, was bumbling and shy, but when he told Jenny that he was happy for her it was clear that he meant every word of it, although it cost him such an effort that he succeeded in ignoring Lord Lamont entirely, while mistaking Sir Simon for someone else and managing somehow to stumble over Lady Carew's feet. Sir Timity, however, rose to the top of his social crest.

"I confess, Sir," he told Oliver, "that if you had not been so quick, I might have stolen this young lady from you. Miss Allen appreciates the cosmopolitan of which type I like to think I am a fine example. You will observe the outfit. Straight down from London on the morning post. Heels quite three inches high! The very pink of fashion. Observe the cut of the pantaloons. Especially designed to creat a certain broadening effect. And if you will only consider this new waistcoat..."

Thus he proceeded to display himself like an undernourished peacock from spindled shank to skinny throat, the latter well hidden by the folds of his cravat.

"I wonder if anything can have happened to Mr. Jackson," Jenny heard Lady Blunder murmur in a distracted way as Sir Timity, certain he had been properly appreciated, pranced off in the direction of refreshments in the company of Mr. Basset. "He means to bring Dr. Dangle with him, you know, my dear, and he assures me we are all to have a great surprise. Ah, my dear Letty! How charming you look in your Leghorn hat. And Captain Walker! Or may I call you David? You must come to see me soon and tell me all about your adventures in America. I have never been precisely certain about what went on there."

"Mama is quite reconciled," Letty said to Jenny under cover of Lady Blunder's loquacity. "David has promised her that if he finds himself in military action in the future, he will take the proper pains, short of desertion, to remain safe."

Just as the two girls embraced, Lady Blunder gave an excited squeal. "There is dear Mr. Jackson!" she was heard to cry. "La, but who is that stranger with him? I thought he meant to bring..."

"Dr. Dangle!" Lady Lamont exclaimed. "Why,

I declare that in the normal way of things I never would have recognized you!"

And, indeed, everyone soon was staring with undisguised amazement at the distinguished gentleman who had arrived in the company of Mr. Jackson.

Dr. Dangle's natural red hair was completely covered by a handsome white powdered wig which looked as though it were made of fox hair. The face beneath had suffered a similar transformation in color, and his eyes were clear and steady as his gait as he came down the gravel path at Mr. Jackson's side. As for his costume, the coal merchant had seen the doctor fitted properly in a blue satin jacket with matching pantaloons and a magnificently embroidered waistcoat. Taken all together, Jenny thought, it was an astonishing sight, particularly when she thought of the doctor as she had last seen him.

"Oh, Mr. Jackson," Lady Blunder cried. "I am sure we all ought to thank you for accomplishing this transformation...."

"Dr. Dangle himself has thanked me to sufficiency, Madam," Mr. Jackson told her with a fond smile.

"Yes, indeed," the doctor said in a stately manner. "I believe I have been quite metamorphosized."

"I declare that I shall miss the old you, although I know I shouldn't," Lady Blunder declared.

"Dear Tabitha, I feel the same," Lady Lamont told her. "There was always something so reassuring about Dr. Dangle's diagnoses. I declare I have never seen anyone make so many without the benefit of an examination."

"And he always had such a profusion of pills and ointments," Lady Blunder wailed, allowing herself to become quite carried away on the waves of fond remembrance.

"Ladies! Ladies!" Dr. Dangle proclaimed, holding up his hands. "Let me set your minds at rest. Physically my condition may have altered but, except in the matter of resisting strong spirits, my character is just the same. I am confident that I can be as poor a doctor sober as I can be drunk."

And on that note the celebrations proceeded. The fiddles played, and there was dancing on the green velvet lawns. Lady Madrigal entertained them with a single song so short as to be nearly endurable. The creams and jellies and other delicacies were attacked with hearty appetites. And, in the silver grey of evening, couples walked beside the river—Lady Carew clinging to Sir Simon's arm, Letty in the shelter of her David's arm, and Lady Blunder with Mr. Jackson at her side.

As for Jenny and Oliver, they were no different than the others, and it came as no surprise to either that their saunter by the river should conclude with a fond embrace.